JOURNEY

TO

MIRAGE

www.BarbartianSpy.com

This book is copyright © habu 2011
Published by BarbarianSpy in 2011.
Cover design by S Bush © 2011
Cover Photo © Ben Goode | Dreamstime.com
All rights reserved.
Ebook ISBN 978-1-921879-13-5
Print ISBN 978-1-921879-14-2

Published by BarbarianSpy an imprint of Cyberworld Publishing
Jindalee St, Toronto, Australia

Barbarian Spy
for Literary Heat

Not all books listed below may currently be on release.

BOOKS BY HABU
Cairo Surrender
Fetish Galore!
Homeward Bound
Journey to Mirage
Choke Hold
Sporting Life

BOOKS BY SHABBU
Operation Black Jade
Cigars!
Angel in the Barn
Gayly Complicated
Despoiling David
The Tree of Idleness
Rough Road to Happiness
I Met a Man
The Interview

BOOKS BY SABB
The Legend of Holleystone Grange
Surprise Encounters
She is He
Wrong Man
Loyal to his King
Barbarian Tales - Book One - Traveler's Tales
Barbarian Tales - Book Two - Journeys Begin
Barbarian Tales - Book Three - The Inheritance
Barbarian Tales - Book Four - Road to Persepolis

BOOKS BY DIRK HESSIAN
Beginning of Time
Prophecy of Noto
The King's Men
Labyrinth

JOURNEY

TO

MIRAGE

habu

Chapter One: Troubleland

Tony had been fidgety all afternoon while Rick and the others were working on stripping down the Mercedes. Tony had said it had been totaled in a wreck and they were to break it down for parts, but it didn't look to Rick like it was in that bad a shape. It was actually a honey of a car, and Rick cringed as he worked to strip the upholstery off the passenger seat— preserving as much of the leather in its original cut as he could.

Rick liked the feel of the leather. In fact, he liked every aspect of working in the auto shop. He thought maybe he'd finally found what he wanted to do in life. He'd known he'd never be a doctor or a lawyer or president of the United States—his family, scraping along in the smoldering inner residential area of Baltimore never had any thoughts of getting ahead that far. The most anyone had aspired to was to own a small pizza joint, like his Aunt Melda did.

His mom was probably as successful as any of them— working as a nurse's aide over at the hospital. And she wanted Rick to go into landscaping.

"An honest, hands-on job out in the fresh air," is the way she'd put it. That's about the best thing Rick could think of that job, though—although it also would help keep him in shape.

But it was cars he liked working with. And he was grateful that Tony had given him this job. At least he was grateful after he'd gotten used to what else Tony gave him, what else Tony wanted from him. It had taken time for Rick to accommodate to that, but now it was something he wanted too. And increasingly Rick thought about it and about Tony being there to satisfy him when he got what Tony called "the itch."

To get close to Tony and to the cars in the shop, Rick had had to close his eyes to some things. Tony obviously was running with some sort of neighborhood gang—in fact was leading it. But he hadn't pressured Rick so far to join with that and some of the things they were doing. Rick didn't know what he'd do if and when Tony came after him to be part of that. He supposed that if it was something Tony wanted him to do, though, that he'd do it. But he wouldn't want to do some of the things the gang was into—at least he'd resist doing it as long as possible.

Today Tony was antsy, though. It had started when those two guys Rick had never seen before came into the auto shop. They looked out of place. They certainly weren't from Rick's mixed Italian and Hispanic neighborhood—the Hispanics pretty much moving in on the Italians, which was one reason there were gangs starting up. Tony was Italian, though, and Rick half Hispanic. This, Rick thought, was why Tony hadn't been quick on trying to bring Rick into the Rumblers.

The two guys who appeared at the garage door were entirely too smooth in Rick's view and were more interested in seeing all that was going on in the shop than was justified with any business they had with Tony.

Tony talked to them at the back of the shop, and from his stance, Rick could tell that Tony wasn't happy about something. The three jawed for about ten minutes and then the two guys left.

That had been a half hour previously. Rick had seen Tony send Marco to the front of the shop, outside the garage doors, which he shut after walking through the door beside them. The shop was in an old warehouse in a compound down by the docks beyond Fells Point that was largely deserted now.

Rick was so busy working on carefully slitting the lacings of the seat leather along the lines it had been already cut, his head down into the passenger compartment of what was quickly becoming a shell of the Mercedes, that he didn't initially notice all the guys around him—all members of the Rumblers and all Italian—putting their tools down and joining Tony at the back of the shop.

He certainly did notice, though, when he heard loud banging from the outside on the steel garage door nearest the door to the street and saw Marco race back into the door, crying out "Cops. Scatter."

Marco was moving fast and Tony and the other Rumblers were close enough to the back to scramble up into the loft of the building and through the hole they'd cut into the neighboring warehouse. None of them tried to leave by the back entrance, which was smart of them, because in short order guys with guns and blue vests started pouring in through that door in addition to the one at the front.

Rick froze—too long to join Tony and the other guys. The best he could do was to crawl into the backseat of the Mercedes shell and try to make himself as invisible as possible.

It was a booming, to be obeyed, voice. "Hey, I see you, kid. Come on out of there—with your hands empty and showin'."

Chapter Two: Baltimore

"I'm off to the grocery store, Ricky. Anything special you want?"

"Hey, give me a couple of minutes to get out of this file and I'll go with you, Mom."

"No, that's OK. You need to finish your homework. I'm gonna stop and get my hair cut too, and there'd be nothing for you to do but kick around the mall. And you know they're cracking down on teenage loiters over there. I don't want you to get into any more trouble—and I want you to stay away from that Rumblers gang, you hear?"

"Yes, Mom, I haven't been near any of those guys since that night. And I'm not a teenager anymore—or at least won't be in another year."

"You know what the judge said," Maxine said, moving to the open doorway to Rick's bedroom so that she could see him and he could see her. Her voice had taken on a sudden note of caution and concern. "He said he was reluctant to let you take auto mechanics at the trade school—that running with those guys from the Rumblers came out of your interest in auto mechanics."

"Geez, Mom. I didn't know they was runnin' a chop shop. They knew their way around cars. I was learnin' a lot."

"Anyway, it's not going to be just the auto mechanics. The judge made that clear. It's good to include the landscaping class—you can help Pete in his business then. That's what the judge thought would be the best for you to do—and Pete is happy with the idea and needs the help—and I think it's quite generous he's willing to pay you as you learn. Don't you think that's good of Pete?"

Rick mumbled something, looking hard into his computer screen while he did so.

"I said, isn't that quite generous of Pete?" Maxine repeated, this time a little louder, and with a touch of irritation in her voice.

"Yeah, Mom, that's great. Pete's a real brick."

"I don't know why you act that way about Pete," Maxine shot back, her voice almost a whisper now. "He's been nothing but good to us. And he's gone out of his way to be nice and friendly to you."

"Yeah, Mom, right."

"You don't know how it is, Ricky. And you aren't the only one around here, young man, with needs and wanting to have a life. I work hard—and so does Pete—you're just lucky the judge let you off from doing any time as long as you had a home to go to. And Pete's offered to let you work with him on the landscaping . . . you know as long as you're on probation, it would be difficult for you to—"

"I said yes, Mom. That it's good of Pete—good of both of you to let me stay here rather than the center. And for Pete to let me work with him."

"So, you'll work to do well in the landscaping class? You won't give all your attention and energy to the auto mechanics? If you'd graduated from high school with your class we wouldn't even be going through this now."

"Yes, Mom."

"And the photography class. That's a possible good hobby for you?"

"Yeah, it's OK, Mom. The instructor's a bit creepy. But the class is OK."

"So, is there anything you need at the grocery store then?"

"Yeah, but it has to be a particular brand. It would be better if I went with you."

11

"I told you it would take you away from your studies too long, Ricky—and I don't want you wandering around in the mall."

"But—"

"You heard your mother, Rick," a gruff voice piped up as a large-framed, big-muscled black guy in tight, weathered jeans and an athletic T loomed into view next to Maxine in the door. Pete instinctively encircled Maxine with an arm and palmed a hand possessively on her belly, and Maxine equally instinctively moved into the contours of his body and laid a hand on top of his. Although Pete's voice was gruff, he was smiling—and Maxine smiled too, her free hand going to wisps of bottle blonde hair around her ears, primping for him as if by habit.

Rick looked at the two of them but then had to look away, burying his eyes once more in the computer screen. Pete was half way between Rick's and Maxine's ages, and Rick could barely stomach how she had worked to make herself seem younger, prettier, sexier even, since Pete had come into her life. Before that she'd been Mom and had acted like one. Now, she was trying so hard to be a sexy lover that in made Rick sick. He wanted a mother, not some slut lusting after a black hunk a good ten years younger than her. Rick knew she'd had it rough since his dad died, but this was pretty ridiculous.

And couldn't she see that was where it had started with him—when his grades had started going downhill so he almost didn't graduate high school and what started him staying out late at night and hooking up with the Rumblers? How could he have stayed at home at night? Her bed—their bed—was just on the other side of the thin wall from his. The sounds, the thumping of the head board against his wall, knowing what Pete was doing to her, and listening to the sounds she made as he did it.

And knowing what else there was. The hell of that. That was the worst of all. No, the worst was that now Rick wanted it—hated himself for wanting it, but wanted it anyway.

"You heard her," Pete repeated. "It isn't convenient for you to go with her. She's going to be gone for a long time—and you have other things to do. We've got a lawn to do tomorrow. I'll drive you by the grocery store then and you can get what you want."

Rick didn't say anything; he just kept on staring into his computer.

"There, isn't that nice of Pete, Ricky? He'll take the time and effort to stop by the grocery store for you tomorrow."

"When you get back, I could—"

"You've got class tonight, and it'll be close to dark and supper time when I get back. And you know the judge said you couldn't drive after dark—without one of us going with you."

Rick said nothing.

"Ricky. I said that's really nice of Pete to offer to do. Tell him thank you, please."

"Thank you, Pete," Rick said, but the voice was low, begrudging, and he didn't look up.

He could hear them kiss. It was quite noisy and sloppy—and, to him, stomach churning.

He didn't look up until he heard the motor start up on his mother's Camaro. And then when he did look up, he was sorry he had. Pete was still in the doorway, filling up the frame with his muscleman body. And he was smiling. And he was unbuckling his belt and pulling down the zipper of his jeans.

* * * *

"Last time we concentrated on landscapes, with black and white photography—mainly Ansel Adams. Tonight, still with black and white, we work on shadows and curves, using the human form," Douglas Groton told the students as they stood around him in the photography studio of the local vocational school in Baltimore's Coppin Heights working-class district. He'd turned off the overhead fluorescents and had spotlights located about the room, all trained on a black-cloth-draped dais, with a bench painted in a black matt finish atop that.

Rick had found Groton to be almost fanatical about his art—or what he called his art. He was teaching this session of the school's photography class because the regular teacher was out on maternity leave, and, although he was full of good and helpful ideas, he acted as if the subject was below him. He minced no words in saying why. This was a class on still photography and he fancied himself a cinematographer. He kept telling the students that this was just a temporary class for him, that he was on his way to a national-level arts film festival and was concentrating his creative efforts on preparing a film entry for that.

Rick thought the guy was a little fanatical in being dismissive of the black and white photography. The Ansel Adams stuff had been really neat. Still, he knew a heck of a lot about still photography and had a lot to say about it—and some fantastical ideas about subject matter and the use of light and angles. Rick thought that if he was saying he was much more into another aspect of the subject than this, he must be a real whirlwind at that.

Rick decided it was the man's eyes. He must have been in his forties and, although not fat, he was definitely on the meaty side. And a hippy type. He dressed minimally, in a T and short shorts and loafers with no socks. And he was dark and hirsute and had a ponytail. Completely out of Rick's concept of a middle-aged white guy. But his eyes. They were a milky blue and, when they turned on a person, they commanded attention. They telegraphed that he was serious and knew what he was doing—and would get his way in doing it.

"And tonight we need a model. I called for some, but it was such short notice. And the human form is what I want to do tonight. So, I guess it will have to be one of us."

Groton's eyes swept the motley group of students hovering around him—but not hovering quite so closely now that he had declared what was needed next. And a motley group it was—mainly middle-aged men and women—clerks and small business accountants and housewives—the type of people taking a kicky hobby night class to forget what they had to face during the workday—and a few late high school-years guys and girls, already bored to tears with life in middle-class Baltimore. None of them looking all that modelish, though.

Except for Rick. He was definitely modelish. His mother wasn't a prize now, but she had been once, and his dad had been a real looker. He'd come up from Cuba to play for the Baltimore Orioles and lasted for just a few seasons on the playing field. But his looks and charm—and connection with professional baseball, albeit tertiary and transitory—had landed him various jobs in small-potato bars and clubs a couple of blocks off the Inner Harbor. This had worked OK for him and his wife and boy until he'd gotten gunned down in a bar robbery.

But he'd been quite a looker—and Rick had taken after him. Not so dusky, thanks to his mother's Scandinavian genes, but permanently tanned and sultry. And he had the natural good physique bestowed honestly by his father's gene pool.

So, Rick looked around in embarrassment with everyone else, but even he noticed that, one after the other, the eyes of each of the other students were coming to rest on him.

"Perhaps you'd do the honors, Mr. Hernandez?"

"Me? Umm, I'm not a model."

"Nor do we have one of those. But what we do have is limited time to get in tonight's class. There's a fee, of course. A model's fee?"

"And what would I have to do?"

"Strip, pose interestingly on the bench on the dais there, and hold the pose regardless of the camera clicks and flashes."

"Strip? I don't—"

"Oh, you can cover any dangly parts with your hands, as you like—as long as it doesn't ruin the pose," Groton said in a throw-away voice that indicated that nothing at all peculiar was being discussed. "And it would be $20 for a half hour's work. Here, if you'll undress I'll help you take a good pose and

15

it will be over almost before it begins. And," the clincher, "since you couldn't be taking photographs at the same time and so couldn't do this assignment, it would be a guaranteed 'A' for this exercise."

Rick needed the "A"—if only to keep his mother and the judge off his back.

Rick dressed as the other students were leaving and Groton was dismantling the set and turning off the spots.

"There, that wasn't so bad, was it?"

"No, no. I guess not. You said there'd be $20?"

"Do you have a way home? Did I hear you tell someone you couldn't drive after dark?"

"Yeah. But I can walk. It's just over on Key."

"That's not all that near. And this isn't the best of neighborhoods. You were a good sport about modeling. I drive by there. I can let you off near your house."

Groton pulled his old Saab over to the side of the street on Scott where Scott crossed Key a block from where Rick said he lived. There was no street light fronting the lot he parked next too. Well, there were street lights, but one was out. The other, struggling to manage by itself, was throwing deep shadows and one beam of fairly strong light that entered the car interior bounced off Rick's lap in the passenger seat and reflected strongly into Groton's eyes from the rearview mirror.

The interesting angle of the light—bringing to Rick's mind several things Groton had told the students earlier about working with light in the photography—caused Rick to look into the rearview mirror—and immediately become entrapped by the look in Groton's eyes as the instructor looked back into Rick's eyes.

"Umm. Thanks for the ride, Mr. Groton. I'll walk from here. It's just over there."

Groton said nothing, made no move that encouraged Rick to make a move either—and held Rick's eyes in thrall with his in the rearview mirror.

"Uh. You said there would be a $20 modeling fee?" Rick asked. He had his hand on the door handle. But he really could use that money—and he couldn't take his eyes off the reflection of Groton's eyes.

"You know, we're given a bit of information on our students, Rick—just to help us know what to expect."

"Uh, do you? That's interesting. If I could just have—"

"I know about your case, Rick. If a student is on probation for something, the instructors are told. So I know about your case. And I know what was reported on how you got involved with that gang leader."

Rick froze in place. He didn't know what to say. The car quite suddenly seemed to be closing in on him. And there were those eyes reflected in the mirror. Knowing eyes. Controlling eyes.

"No problem with the $20, Rick. But another $20 can be had if you let me hold you."

Rick didn't say anything. Not being fully sure what Groton was saying—asking, offering. At least hoping he didn't understand. But with the next thing Groton said, Rick fully understood.

"And another $10 if you come for me while I'm holding it."

Rick said nothing. He began to tremble, and he managed to wrest his gaze away from the rearview mirror. But that was mostly at the sound of his zipper being lowered.

But not saying anything also meant he didn't object or say "no" or do anything really other than feel powerless and hopeless and having no control over his limbs—especially not the one being drawn out of his jeans now and being squeezed and slowly pumped, the one coming to life under the touch of Groton's long, sensitive, artistic hand.

"You just said hold it," he squeaked.

"Do you really want me to stop?"

Silence.

Rick's gaze latched onto his lap, where the beam of light from the overhead streetlamp focused his attention on his engorging cock and Groton's moving fist.

"See how exciting the play of light can be?" Groton whispered, shaping and sharpening and giving focus to the thoughts that were also playing around in the back of Rick's mind—below the surface of his urge to resist and his frustration at the weakness not to be able to. And at the disgust at himself for responding to this, wanting it.

"I parked here on purpose, Rick," Groton said. "You were such a good model tonight that I wanted you to understand what we were studying at an even greater depth—in a way you'd never forget."

Groton made it sound almost reasonable—academic—detached from what was actually happening in the car. And natural and OK. Almost.

Rick tore his gaze away from his lap, but he made the mistake of looking into the rearview mirror again—where Groton's eyes captured his again and held them.

Rick whimpered and felt his hips involuntarily moving—rising to meet the downward slow pump of Groton's fist. He felt he was close to coming. Groton's heavy breathing wasn't helping. Rick knew Groton wanted him. Rick wanted to be wanted. If Groton asked him now to fondle him, or jack him off, or suck him, or even to open his legs for him now, right here in this car, Rick would have done so. Just like he'd done for Tony and any other Rumbler Tony had designated.

But Groton didn't do any of those things. He laughed and took his hand away from Rick's cock. He opened the glove compartment of the car and pulled two twenties out, folded, and extended them across the seat to Rick.

Rick had seen that there were only the two twenties in the glove compartment. And it dawned on him that Groton was teasing him. All part of a game of control.

"Maybe next time," Groton said. And then he laughed again, as Rick fumbled with getting his cock back in his jeans and zipping them up with one hand and getting the car door open with the other so that he could stumble out onto the crumbling concrete sidewalk under the beam of the one streetlight.

Groton was still laughing when he pulled away from the curb.

The streetlights were all working on Key, and Rick, his senses sparking with electricity, saw, with new eyes, the play of the shadows on the slight concave curve of the townhouse fronts—a long row of two-story brick fronts with identical highly scrubbed and white-washed stoops with two steps to the street from the identically cut front doors.

He was trying to concentrate on how Groton had opened his eyes to an image like this—determined now to catch it on film himself—perhaps unconsciously trying to obliterate or soften the humiliation he had just experienced, when his attention was arrested by the flashing of red lights. On the street, right across the sidewalk from where his own front door would be.

As he came closer to his house, his mother's Camaro turned out of the parking space and chugged into the street. What Rick immediately felt was relief. His mother and Pete must be going out clubbing. They wouldn't be back until well after midnight, then. A night of peace and quiet for him.

But when he opened the door, there was Pete, across the room, coming out of the kitchen, a football game showing on the television in the living room and a beer can in his hand. He was wearing sleeping shorts—and nothing else. And he was a pile of perfectly formed ebony muscle.

"Oh," Rick said. "The Camaro. I thought—"

"The hospital called. Two aides called in sick. They offered Maxine double time to work the night shift."

"Oh."

"So, we're home alone."

Rick knew what that meant. "Well, you've got a game. And I've got some schoolwork to—"

"You look like you want it. You look like you want it bad."

Rick had no idea how Pete could tell. But he couldn't say Pete was wrong.

"Come upstairs. My room."

19

"Not in mother's bed. No, I couldn't—"

"Oh, I think you can," Pete said. Then he laughed as he put a big mitt on Rick's shoulder and guided him toward the stairs.

Rick groaned and arched his back, his fists grabbing at the slats of the headboard of his mother's bed. Pete was kneeling, facing him, between his legs, his knees and thighs forced under and lifting Rick's buttocks, giving Pete a clear channel for his favorite entrance—and for his straight, smooth, but forced, if necessary, nine-inch, rock-hard slide. It drove Maxine crazy. It didn't do much less for her son.

"Tell me you want it," Pete muttered, the bulb of his cock caressing the rim of Rick's channel, ready to strike.

Rick might have been satisfied. He had come quickly when Pete opened his mouth over his cock and pulled it inside his throat. But he wasn't satisfied. That was what Tony had done to him. Made him want it. But Tony wasn't hung like Pete was.

"Yes." It was a mere whisper.

"Yes, what?"

"Yes, I want it. Ple—. Oh, gawd, oh gawd, oh fuccccck." Rick's knuckles went white from his death grip on the slats of the headboard and he turned his head to the side and bit into a pillow, his nose taking in the unmistakable scent of his mother's perfume as Pete began his long slide inside. And then Rick gasped and tried to widen his legs further, as the sound of the bed frame rhythmically beating a tattoo against his bedroom wall commenced its music of the night.

He was deep into the fuck himself now. Wanting it. Meeting thrust for thrust as Pete grunted and laughed. "See, you're a natural. You want to have it as bad as I want to take it. You're a little slut. But I can pull out now. I can stop giving it to you. You want that?"

"Nooo," Rick pleaded. "No, all of it, deep please. Fuck me!"

Chapter Three: Fantasyland

"You said you'd take me by the grocery store for what you wouldn't let me go with Mom to get yesterday."

"Got this job at the other side of town that just got called in, Rick. You can walk home from here after you mow this guy's lawn and trim those hedges over there—although neither job looks like it needs doing real bad. Tell me what you want from the grocery and I'll pick it up for you when I'm finished cross town. This double pay will do us real well."

"No, thanks," Rick said. "I'll get it another time." It was nonsensical for him to reject the offer, and Rick knew it was. But it was the only rejection Rick was able to make toward this man who should be his father figure but who was banging both Rick's mother and Rick—with each one of them addicted to what Pete gave them.

Rick watched Pete drive off in the truck after Pete told him not to worry about payment for this job—that the guy had prepaid—and then he restarted the mower and tried to remember where he'd left off on the front yard. Pete had been right, the lawn didn't look like it needed to be mowed; Rick could hardly tell where he'd mowed already and where he hadn't.

He did a few more rows, which brought him back to where he was looking directly at the front porch—and then he stopped dead in his tracks, taking his hand off the throttle and letting the mower die.

"Take your T-shirt off and continue mowing. There's $20 extra in it for you—money you don't have to report to anyone."

"Why?" Rick asked, both confused and belligerent.

Doug Groton was standing at the top of the steps, at the edge of the covered porch. All he had on was a pair of short shorts. He was holding a camera in one hand and was leaning against a post and giving Rick a half-sneering smile.

"Because I want to photograph you in action. I want to get young muscle shots."

"This yard doesn't really need to be mowed," Rick said, standing there dead in his tracks. "You're wasting your money."

"Not if I get some good photos out of this. You have no idea what they'll pay in galleries for interesting specialty shots. I supply a special gallery where photos like ones of you mowing a yard will sell like hotcakes."

"The yard doesn't really need mowed," Rick repeated doggedly.

"Then if you're interested in making another fifty and come inside for a more private photo shoot, no one will know you weren't spending the time mowing the yard, will they?"

"You didn't need your yard mowed, did you?"

"Bingo. But you should give me points for tracking down your friend's lawn service."

"He's not my friend," Rick said.

"Does he fuck you?"

Rick said nothing. So, Groton didn't really need for him to answer.

"Does he fuck you good? He looks like he's hung low and he looks strong enough to go all day. I'd like to get some specialty photos of him too. And of the two of you together."

Rick said nothing. There was nothing much he could say.

"Do you want the $20? It's not like men don't mow their lawns without their shirts on. What's the problem with that? I'll bet every kid mowing a lawn in Baltimore today is doing it shirtless. I'm surprised I even had to ask. And I won't bite—even if you want the fifty and come inside for an hour or two."

Rick did want the twenty—and the fifty too. And he was much too naïve to even think about his photos being sold in galleries like Groton was hinting they would be—or have any inkling how paltry those fees were against what Groton could make with multiple copies of the photos.

Inside the house, in Groton's basement, Rick was awed at the professional equipment and staging area Groton had set up down there. Once again the velvet-covered dais, like in the night school building, but here there was a dark blue velvet drape behind it as well and a brocade chaise lounge on the dais.

"You want me to strip completely down? I don't know—"

"What's the problem? You've already done it for the photography class."

"But I was permitted to—"

"Don't be silly. I've already handled it. For fifty I'm going to want you to jack it off."

"While you are taking photos?"

"Yep. Both video and stills. But I'll tell you what, if you are that shy and will take just $30, I have a mask you can wear. Nobody you know will see these anyway. These will just be art shots. You've seen my photographs. You'll look good."

"I don't . . ." Rick just ran down, and Groton didn't fill in the blanks for him. Rick really wanted that extra $50.

But after nearly a minute, Groton said. "Hey, I won't even touch you—unless you want me to—and then I'd add money to the pot. I'll just take some pose-shot stills and then I'll let you do yourself while I video and take other stills."

"I don't know if I can."

"I'll help you. I'll lead you into some fantasy talk that will help you. It's not a problem. I've done this before. So, do you want me to bring out a mask?"

"No. I'll do the $50 shoot."

"Do you want me to help you get those shorts off."

"No. You said you wouldn't—"

"Well, the clock's ticking. So, if we're going to do this, you need to strip and get up on that couch."

For a half hour, as Rick posed this way and that, as Groton instructed, the only sounds in the room were the clicking of the camera and Groton's breathy expressions. As the shoot went on, Groton became increasingly hands on with setting the poses. But it happened so gradually that Rick didn't object until Groton was sitting beside him while Rick was stretched out on the chaise and had a hand encircling Rick's cock. Groton's gaze, however, was plastered to Rick's face through the camera lens in a close-up.

"Hey, you said you won't—"

"Another $20? These are going to be great shots—of your facial expressions as I'm masturbating you—except you can't come. We just want you worked up big for the video. It's no more than I did with you in my car. Just relax. I won't fuck you—unless you want me too. Just a hand job and not all the way. For an extra twenty bucks."

Rick sighed and tried to relax, which wasn't easy with the camera in his face and Groton muttering how nice he was and what a natural model he was.

"Now," Groton said at length, when he thought he'd gotten the length out of Rick's cock that he wanted, "for the video." He popped up and went behind one of three cameras and turned it on and made adjustments and then went to the other two in succession, so that they were all rolling film.

"What do you want me to—?"

"Just lay back and masturbate and respond to my questions—hold it as long as you can, but then go ahead and let it fly. And don't hold back on your reactions. Just like you were alone and thinking the things we're talking about. Natural, but be expressive too. Nothing phony, though. You're sweet and young and hung and cut and have a great face. That's what will sell."

Rick took his cock in his hand and started to slowly pump.

"You like being fucked by black men? Black men with muscles and long, thick cocks?"

"No," Rick answered quickly.

"Nothing phony, son. I can see your cock liked the question. I think we both know that big black stud nails you. And that gang leader Tony too. And how many in his gang? You like ethnic? There, see, you can get harder. Relax and let true arousal take you. That black guy you work with. He pins you to the floor with a big one, doesn't he?"

"Yes," given reluctantly, after a pause.

"And you want it despite some reservations? Right."

Another pause and then a "yes."

"What is it? The blackness? The muscles? The big cock? The domination? The fact you shouldn't be doing it but know you want it?"

After some thought, "All of that, I guess."

"What are your fantasies of being taken?"

"My fantasies?"

"Yes. Like athletes. Black athletes. Muscles, big cocked . . . you continue with that, if it's something you dream about."

Rick didn't respond right away, but Groton could see that he was giving the question some thought, so he stopped crowding the young man. At length, Rick started talking in a dreamy voice.

"Just coming off the field. Hot and sweaty. On the bench in the locker room. Him tonguing the sweat off me."

"Yes, yes, go on. And then fucking you on the bench?"

"Yes, yes. But then moving on, on the field this time, jersey and shoulder pads still on but each naked below the waist. On the bleachers—nearly dark, but not quite, my ankles on his shoulders. Too much, almost too big, but he just . . . continues . . . ohh, sorry, you said to try to . . . but—"

"No, that's just fine," Groton said as he moved around shutting down cameras and turning off spot lights. "That was a very nice ejaculation. And now that you have the hang of it, start thinking of another scenario as you rebuild."

"Again? You didn't say—"

25

"I didn't say just once. But just one more this afternoon. Then I'll give you, what, $90 for today, isn't it? Then you can think it over and think of other fantasies of yours and I'll pay you $50 for each climaxed session then. How does that sound?"

"Just one more today, and you'll give me $90?"

"If you don't think about it too long, I'll make it $100 for today's work. How much do you make in two hours for mowing people's lawns—plus the manual labor under the hot sun?"

Twenty minutes later, Groton clicked the cameras and lights back on.

"Have you formed another fantasy."

"No, not completely. Something perhaps about running through a meadow—pursued."

"By one or several?"

Rick closed his eyes and contemplated.

"No, continue stroking, please. Always continue stroking through this. One or several. Several, right? That arouses you—more than one."

"Yes, several."

Now it was Groton's time to contemplate. But only for a moment. "Have you seen the movie *Deliverance*?"

"Yes."

"Gave you a hard on?" And then, without waiting for an answer, "You are being chased through a meadow."

"Before that," Rick now took over the story as he stroked. "I'm driving down the line of mountains, wanting to cross them, and have turned into a road I think leads to a pass. But it doesn't, it just goes farther back in a fold in the mountains, into a small valley. I've made several turns and now don't know which way to go. I stop at a log cabin that has smoke coming from its chimney. It's beside a meadow. I get out of my car and go up to the door and knock."

"And the man who answers is nearly naked," Groton says. "You have caught him fucking another man—all men from the mountains—and there were other men watching."

26

"Yes, yes," Rick said. "Wait. I'll go on but I need to stroke slower, I'm about to—"

"Yes, don't stop, but you can fight for control."

After a brief moment, "I start to say I'm lost. But then I see the expressions on their faces and realize what I have walked into. I turn and begin running. One of them dashes out of the door—a big bruiser of a man—and cuts me off from reaching my car."

"Yes, yes. Go on."

"I turn toward the only avenue they give me—out through a gate in a fence running alongside the cabin."

"And into the meadow."

"Yes, into the meadow. I am running as fast as I can. But they are men of the mountain, used to the hard life. Barefoot, but all running faster than I am."

"But they don't catch you right away."

"No, they are teasing me, toying with me. Leaving an avenue that I think may allow me to escape. But closing the gap, circling around me, getting closer and closer."

"And then?"

"And then I drop in exhaustion and they are upon me like vultures. And tearing at my clothes. Laughing as they strip me naked. Tearing my clothes like I'll not need them again."

"And that terrifies you? That they don't care if you won't have any clothes after this? Like maybe you'll have no need for clothes?"

"Yes." It was a mere whisper.

"And are they saying anything to each other while they're doing this?"

Rick paused for a moment, but then he continued in a small, hoarse voice—obviously close to coming. "Yes, they are joking with each other on how each is going to take me. And . . . and . . ."

"Yes, and?"

"And the big bruiser is telling them that they need to go in order of size, smallest to largest, which would put him last. That they need to stretch me progressively."

"And they do take you in succession?"

"Yes."

"And you can feel them inside you?"

"No. I feel nothing like that. It's a dream. I have no feeling sense. But I know what they're doing. Their faces are close to mine. I can see in their eyes what they're doing to me."

"And the big bruiser is last and has a monster cock."

"Yes."

"You don't feel it, though?"

"No. But he makes me watch—down the line of my body—while he stuffs it in."

"But that's not all, is it Rick? You haven't come. There's more."

"Yes," Rich said in a faraway, breathy voice.

"More than one takes you together, don't they? . . . Ah, yes, that was a nice one. Even nicer than the first."

Groton moved around his cameras and lights, turning them off, and humming in self-satisfaction.

"There's a shower in through there. I'll have your money when you come back. You are a delightful model. All you have to do is decide you will do other sessions and we're in business."

* * * *

Rick was so deep in thought as he walked home from Groton's house, his fist wrapped around the five crisp twenty-dollar bills in his shorts pocket, that he didn't hear the low-rider 1959 Chevy Impala glide up beside him.

"Where ya' goin'? Come inside. We'll take you home."

Rick turned and backed up a step. "Can't be seen with you, Tony. You know that. I'm on probation. No hard feelings, but can't be seen with you."

"Ah, com'on, climb in. Nobody will see you. Course they might see you just standin' out there and talkin' with me. That's what could get you in trouble. Hidden in here won't get you in trouble. It's safer in the car than out."

"Tony, please . . ."

"Forgotten me already? Used to be all I had to do was tell you to spread your legs and you were all over me. Nope, you can start walkin' again"—which is what Rick had turned toward home and started to do—"but I'll ride right along beside you—for the whole neighborhood to see we're together again. Com'on, you need some of what I can give you again. Climb in. We'll let you loose far enough from home that no one will be the wiser."

"Please, Tony . . ."

But when the back door of the Chevy opened, Rick shrugged, looked around, and climbed aboard.

There were two Latinos he didn't know in the backseat, and as he entered, the one sitting beside the door he entered pulled him right on across and sat him down between them. They each had an arm around his shoulders and their free hands were feeling and unbuttoning and unzipping before the door was completely shut and the Chevy glided off into the street.

Tony turned in the front passenger seat and gave Rick a sharp look. "Don't do that, Rick. Just stop struggling. This here is Hosea 1 and over there is Hosea 2. That's all you need to know. They're suppliers of mine and I've been tellin' them what a sweet ass you have. Favor for favor. You just cooperate and maybe I don't cruise in your neighborhood so much. No one sees us together; no one tells your probation officer."

Then, as Rick settled down, Tony turned to the driver and said, "Find a nice quiet neighborhood. Not much activity, trees meetin' overhead. We'll open the skylight and let Rick enjoy the view."

Rick didn't get to see the view, though, because as one of the Latinos lapped him, the other was on his knees and pulling Rick's mouth down to his cock. Then they reversed positions.

"Oh lookee here," Tony said from the front seat as they were driving back to Rick's neighborhood. "Where'd you get $100. Been whorin' down in the harbor?" He held Rick's shorts in one hand and the roll of twenties in the other.

"I earned that. Put it back," Rick said.

"Oh, snappish are we? I was thinkin' on taking you back to the garage for a little party, but I'll just take this instead. And you won't see me around for a while. That sound good to you?"

Rick mumbled that it did. There wasn't much else he could do. He was in despair, though. Not only was he out money he needed to get out of Baltimore, but he saw now that Tony wasn't finished with him—and would be a threat as long as Rick was under probation not to be seen with him.

And at the same time, he was frustrated, because all the time the two Latinos were fucking him, he was wishing that it was Tony—and, worse, Pete. He had thought he had escaped that addiction, but he realized now that he was wrong. He knew now that as soon as he went off probation he'd be right back in Tony's garage and bed—if Tony would have him. Now, more than before, getting out of Baltimore was his only out.

That night, as he lay in bed, listening to his mother's squeals and moans as the headboard of Pete and her bed just across the wall from Rick's own bed beat a steady rhythm against his head, Rick thought about how he was going to get more money. By the time the house had gone quiet, he realized that the only way short of stealing it was to go back to Groton's house for more sessions.

Late in the night, he was awakened by the groan of his mattress as Pete's heavy body lowered on his.

"Pete . . . no," Rick murmured as he felt the hand at the waistband of his sleeping shorts, pulling them down and off his legs. And then knees and heavily muscled thighs were pushing between his legs.

"You want it. You know you want it," Pete whispered in a gruff voice. "Give it to me. Open to me."

Thick fingers were invading Rick's channel, and he moaned and began to move his hips in involuntary surrender.

This was another reason he had to leave Baltimore. Pete was right. Rick wanted him.

The light by his bed went on.

"Why—"

"I thought something special tonight. I want to watch it goin' in—and out and in again. And I want you to watch it too. You're gonna love watchin' it work."

Rick moaned.

Rick felt the grip of Pete's fists on his ankles, and he groaned has his legs were raised and hooked on Pete's tight-muscled shoulders.

And then as Pete's cock head fumbled at Rick's hole, Rick reached down with both hands and guided the cock home. Pete laughed a deep, throaty laugh and thrust home, as Rick reached up and grabbed for the brass rods of his headboard, trying to pull it toward him so it wouldn't bump against the wall in rhythm to Pete's thrusts and reverberate in his mother's room. Pete slapped Rick's legs off his shoulders and cupped his buttocks and lifted his pelvis so Rick could look down the line of his body and see the thick, three-quarters buried cock. Rick moaned again as he saw the cylinder moving in and out of him.

Then he closed his eyes and fantasized about being on the bleachers on a football field in the twilight and a young, black, hung, muscled, athletic stud fucking him to ecstasy.

Chapter Four: Perplexityland

Rick's mother schlepped into the kitchen in just a mint-green hospital smock and fluffy bedroom slippers. She took a searching, not altogether approving, look at her son, hunched over a cereal bowl, textbooks fanned out around him. Then she moved to the counter beside the refrigerator, took up a half-empty package of cigarettes she found there, and lit a cigarette with a match from a matchbook that had been lodged in the cigarette package. She turned, leaning the small of her back against the counter, and took a puff of the cigarette, holding the cigarette to her mouth with one hand, the arm of which she supported with her other hand on the elbow.

Rick looked up and scowled at her and then hunched back over his cereal bowl and the books. He wished she wouldn't walk around the house like that. The hospital smock was flimsy and it showed every contour of her curvy body, including, notably, the swell of her stomach and the protrusions of her bullet-sized nipples.

"Is that your homework you're doing?"

"Yes ma'am."

"Weren't you supposed to be doing that yesterday afternoon?"

"Yep, but I was out on a lawn job. Pete sent me. You can ask him, if you want."

"I wouldn't bother," she said, as she blew out a ring of smoke and took another drag on the cigarette. "He always takes up for you. Which is why I don't know why you're so down on him."

"Mom, I gotta study. There's a test today in the auto mechanics course."

"You should be studying the landscaping course more than that one. I've gotten reports you're lagging in that."

"I want to be an auto mechanic, Mom."

"So you can run around with Tony and his gang again?"

"No, of course not. And please don't start ragging on me about that again."

"Sandra told me she saw you talkin' to Tony through his car window the other day. She said Pete saw you too, but when I asked him, he wouldn't say he saw you. You know that—"

Rick sat up in his chair then and snapped one of the books shut—obviously to show irritation.

"Mom, let's get out of Baltimore. Let's move out West someplace where it's entirely different. Dry and with clean air. How about someplace like Santa Fe? They got cars there I could work on and you can get a job in a hospital almost anywhere."

"And what would the judge who has you on probation say to that, son? You think he'd just let you waltz off out of his jurisdiction like that?"

"We can ask. My next appointment with my probation office is coming right up. It would be a clean break of the Baltimore and what's happened here. I think he'd agree that movin' on would be a good move. That's what they say they want me to do—make a clean break from the influences I got going on here."

"Autos needing fixed and patients needing taking care of are easy enough, Ricky. But what about Pete? What sort of landscaping do they need—grass cutting—in a desert?"

"That's one of the points, Mom. Pete wouldn't come. We'd make a clean break of it."

Maxine was seeing red now. She stood away from the counter and turned and viciously ground out her half-smoked cigarette in an ash tray nearly overflowing with earlier cigarettes, put her hands on her hips, and lashed out. "I've had about enough of that talk about Pete now. He's the best thing that's happened to this house since your father. You resent him because he's black—and younger than me. Don't you?"

"No, Mom, that's not any part of it. There's stuff you need to know—stuff I don't know why you don't know already."

"I don't want to hear any of your *stuff* about Pete. You just don't want to see me happy. And you resist accepting Pete no matter what he does for you—the lawn business and all—and how much attention he pays to you."

"Attention is right," Rick said through a snort. "About that fuckin' atten—"

"You just . . . shut . . . your mouth about—"

"Oh, Christ, I give up," Rick nearly shouted in frustration. Then he stood, sending his cereal bowl, still with an inch of milk at the bottom, and the spoon clattering to the floor, as he brutally gathered his textbooks and stumbled out of the kitchen.

He went to his room and dressed for his classes. He was expected at Groton's this afternoon. He'd barely have time to race through that test on auto mechanics and run over to Groton's to get there when he was expected.

The sounds from the kitchen arrested his race for the front door, however, as he passed from the bedrooms to the front of the house. He paused just long enough to see that Pete was in the kitchen now. He had Maxine backed up to the counter, with the flimsy hospital smock bunched up around her waist. Pete's hands were under the smock and obviously covering Maxine's pendulous breasts. And although he was wearing long, cotton sleeping pants, there was no mystery what was protruding from the fly and was buried half way up Maxine's cunt. Rick could actually see the root of the cock and a good inch and a half—disappearing and then appearing again.

Just like what Pete had made him watch when Pete was fucking him. From the sounds Maxine was making, she was loving every stroke of it. Rick reddened up at the thought that he'd loved every stroke of it too.

In disgust and frustration, Rick slammed the front door behind him hard as he left the house and raced down the porch steps to the sidewalk. He'd have just about enough time to catch the bus headed for school before his landscaping class started.

* * * *

Rick's appointment with Douglas Groton had been set through Pete the day before.

"Mr. Groton over on Maple called and said his grass needed cut again and that he liked the way you did it last time and asked for you specifically to cut it tomorrow afternoon, about four."

Rick looked hard at Pete to determine if there was any question there why Groton had asked for him specifically, but Pete was busy watching an Orioles baseball game, so Groton's timing was better than he imagined it would be. Pete didn't want to leave the game anyway, so he didn't give the request much thought. He was too far into the six pack of beer he was guzzling to think too clearly about anything. Rick knew he'd be out like a light tonight and was unlikely to pay a visit to Rick's room.

Rick couldn't wait to get out the door of his auto mechanics test and down the block to the bus stop. Luckily the test had been a snap—even though he was almost hyperventilating through it in anticipation of getting to Groton's house by four. It was four days past the time he'd resolved that he wanted Groton's money and was prepared to do just about anything to get it. He'd also been thinking of scenarios that were arousing and discovered that there actually were a few he often latched into.

Groton was waiting for him on the porch of his house. Rick noticed that, unlike his last visit, the yard actually needed to be mowed this time.

"You been thinking about what I offered?" Groton said as he rose out of a rattan chair on the porch and moved into the sunshine at the edge of steps.

"Yes, I have, Mr. Groton."

"And?"

"I'm interested. And I've been thinking of stories."

"OK, good. The mower is around by the garage. Mow the yard, please."

"Mow the yard?"

"Yes."

"You want me to strip off my T or anything?"

"No, I'd like you to leave it on today. I won't be taking photos out here. Want to watch you get good and sweaty, though."

"It's sure the day for it. I'll bet it hits 100."

"I hope so. Don't dawdle in getting it mowed, though. I have plans for your time. A hundred for two hours of work OK with you?"

"Yeah. I guess. To do what, though, in addition to mowing the yard."

"Anything I want. Without complaint. I finish satisfied and there will be an additional fifty in it for you. OK?"

"Yeah. Yeah, I guess so." Rick really needed the money.

It was a scorcher and both Rick's T and his shorts were soaked flat against his body when he was done. Groton had let him have water, but he'd driven him to mow fast and not take a breather break. Rick was panting when he finished.

"I changed my mind about photos," Groton said as he came down off the porch with a camera when Rick had put the mower away and came back into the front yard.

"Stand there, please. Chest out and, no, don't try covering your basket."

Groton circled Rick, clicking off photos. Then he started climbing the steps again. "Come into the house, please."

"Should I towel off or something before I walk through your house?" Rick asked.

"Not a chance. Just come in and go on down to the basement."

Rick did a double take when he entered the photo studio. He just stood there and gaped, while Groton went around adjusting his three video cameras and turning on spotlights.

"What's this? It looks like a locker room," Rick murmured. A rough wood bench sat on the dais backdropped by a semicircle of lockers like you'd find in a sports locker room.

"Yes, that's the effect I was after. Here, strip off the shorts and jock, but leave the T on. And pull these on."

Rick took the old-style hip pads and flimsy football pants Groton handed him. "Uh, what—?"

"No time for questions. And here, let me introduce you to Spike. He's going to help with this photo shoot."

Rick's eyes snapped around to take in a hulking black guy who was already outfitted in old-style hip pads half-covered by tight-fitting football pants—and nothing else. His ebony muscles piled up over a thick, but by no means fat, armor plate of washboard abs. His biceps alone looked thicker than Rick's waist. He had a strong-featured face and dreadlocks that dipped down to his shoulders. He was giving Rick a "I could eat you all up" look.

"Go ahead. Dress," Groton commanded.

"I don't under—"

"Your fantasy. The last time you were here, Rick. The locker room fantasy. There's a method to this. You do this right and I'll tell you what it is. It would mean good money for you."

"But this guy? What—?"

37

"Spike's going to help you play out that fantasy, Rick. He's going to fuck you silly, just like in your fantasy. And I'm going to get it on film. Consider this your screen test for big bucks. Or do you want to take the forty for mowing the yard and go home now?"

"Fuck me? I can't—"

"Are you going to go back to pretending he'd be the first big black cock inside you? You want the money? We don't have all day. Strip."

Rick only hesitated briefly before he stripped off his shorts and jock and tied the old-fashioned football hip pads around his waist with trembling hands and pulled on the pants, which turned out to be made of some sort of flimsy, silky material.

Then Groton got behind the cameras, made a few adjustments, and said. "OK, Spike, do it like I told you to. Rick, you can struggle a bit at first if you want, but the camera wants to see you surrender and then want it. OK, go."

Rick didn't have to do anything. Spike merely walked over to him, put an arm around his shoulder and guided him onto the lighted set like they were returning to the locker room from football practice. He stopped between the bench and the camera and pulled Rick's sweaty T over his head and lowered his thick lips to Rick's chest and began licking the sweat off him. They were more or less joined at the hip, showing three quarters of their bodies to the camera. Spike was encircling Rick's waist with one arm, and Rick arched back to give the camera a good shot of Spike licking Rick's nipples and up into his pits in turn. And then Spike started working his tongue down Rick's chest and over his belly. With his free hand, he ripped open the tight football pants at the waist and slowly unlaced the hip pads covering Rick's pelvis. By the time his lips reached Rick's lower belly, Spike was on his knees and his hand was drawing out Rick's cock. Spike sucked briefly on Rick's freed balls before closing his lips over Rick's cock and beginning to give him suck.

Rick trembled in Spike's controlling embrace and licked his lips and moaned and groaned in response to the working of Spike's mouth and tongue. This indeed was one of his fantasies and he just gave in to it.

At length, Spike stood and guided Rick over to the bench, pushing the young man down into a seated position straddling one end of the bench. Spike, also straddling the bench, stood in front of Rick and slowly split his tight pants to below his crotch, fanned out the two sides, and languidly unlaced his hip pads and let his heavy cock and balls drop between his legs. Rick opened his eyes wide—caught neatly by the cameras—and moaned, as Spike palmed the back of Rick's head with his hands and guided Rick's mouth to his cock.

When he was ready, Spike stood away from the bench, turned Rick over, belly to bench, still straddling the bench. He went down to his knees at the end of the bench, palmed Rick's butt cheeks with his two hands and separated the two orbs, showing Rick's now-pulsing hole.

Rick groaned as Spike blew on the hole and then he began to pant and moan as Spike's mouth and tongue went to the entrance. After a few minutes, Spike was standing and moving over Rick and presenting his monstrously thick cock head to Rick's hole and slowly feeding it inside and Rick was crying out and writhing under him—all caught beautifully by the cameras.

The fuck was all that Rick had fantasized about. He gripped the legs of the bench hard, and, with his pelvis slightly raised and presented to the best angle for Spike's pumping cock, Rick's own cock head rubbed across the rough wood of the bench and he came a long time before Spike was finished. At Groton's direction, he had turned his head to the side, looking into the cameras, so they could catch every nuance of what Spike's cock was doing inside him.

And then Groton was standing by the bench, tugging at Spike, who pulled out of Rick and stepped to the side. The cameras were still rolling. Groton turned an exhausted Rick over on his back, still straddling the bench with his quivering legs.

Groton stood over Rick at the end of the bench, his own legs straddling the end, and he smiled down at Rick as he unzipped his pants and flared the sides out. Rick watched in awe as the photographer pulled out the longest cock he'd ever seen. It wasn't thick, but it was a good ten inches.

"Remember, I said anything I wanted you to do during the session," Groton said, that smile nearly a sneer.

"I don't know. It's so . . . ohhh, holy shit. Ohhhhh."

Groton entered him forever and ever, way up inside Rick's channel, while he held Rick's leg away from the cameras up and out and the other leg at a down and out angle, so that the cameras got the full view of him entering, entering, entering. Rick arched his back, trying to get as much of a straight angle up into him that he could give that pole of a cock. And groaned and moaned.

"This is one of *my* fantasies, Rick," Groton whispered. Then he laughed, and began a long-stroking pumping that had Rick panting and shuddering with each deep stroke.

And the cameras whirred away.

* * * *

"I'm in a bathtub, leaning back at one end. Facing me, leaning against the opposite end, is another man."

"Young or old? No, don't open your eyes. And move your hand away. Let me do it."

"Neither. But he is beefy. And with a thick matting of hair on his chest and his arms. The rest is under the water. But I keep my eyes on the wet, curly black hair. And his has a tight, curly black beard too—and black hair falling down to his neck."

"Is he handsome?"

"Not really. There's a scar slicing down from his hairline to where his beard starts on his cheek. But it's a strong face."

It was a week later than the locker room sequence, and Rick had been called to mow Douglas Groton's yard again. They were upstairs, on Groton's bed. Both naked. Both stretched out on their backs, but Rick overlapping one of Groton's legs and an arm. Groton's free hand was encircling Rick's cock and slowly pumping. Two cameras, focused on the bed, were whirring at different angles in the room. This time the lighting was more subtle—Groton was working with shadows. But there was a spotlight beamed on Rick's pelvis, making sure that Groton's masturbation of Rick was clearly seen by the cameras.

"That's all? You're just sitting there, in a tub of bath water, facing each other?"

"No, that's not all."

"What's going on below the waterline, Rick?"

"He is sitting on the bottom of the tub."

"And what are you sitting on, Rick?"

"His . . . his . . ."

"You're sitting on his cock, aren't you? Your butt cheeks are on his thighs, right?"

"Yes. Silky thighs. Hairy there, too, but felt more than seen. He is in me thick and deep. Rocking back and forth, making small waves in the water."

"Where are his hands?"

"One is around my waist, palming the small of my back, holding me to him."

"And where is the other?"

"He has his middle finger inside me—in my channel. Rubbing against my prostate, running along the top of the cock he has inside me."

"And how does that make you feel?"

"My balls ache. He keeps at it. I've come at least twice. The water is cloudy from my come."

"You haven't asked him to stop?"

"No, I never want him to stop."

"And where are your hands?"

"One below us, on his balls. The other working myself. Oh, god, Doug. I think . . . I'm . . . going to come."

"Of course you are." Groton moved down Rick's body. His mouth now covering Rick's cock and his hand going to Rick's hole, the middle finger searching out his prostate and rubbing. Until, with a shudder and a lurch, Rick came.

Groton held Rick close in an embrace while Rick's ragged breathing became more regular. Rick liked this as much as anything Groton did to and for him. Pete always pulled out immediately after getting his own pleasure and was gone, leaving Rick spun out and grasping for some sign of affection in the act.

After Groton felt Rick relax and close to sleep, he spoke. "Tell me, Rick—truthfully—why you need this money I'm paying you. I didn't see enthusiasm to my advances. What I saw was a need. And I think it was a need for funds."

"I need to get out of Baltimore."

"But you're on probation."

"That's one of the main reasons I need to leave. I'll lose the probation if I associate with the gang that got me into trouble in the first place. And they won't leave me alone. They think it's funny to keep me on the edge."

"And that's all."

A pause and than a somewhat tentative, "Yes."

"That's not really all, is it?"

"No."

"Have anything to do with that big black stud you work with and who fucks you?"

"Yes. But I don't want to get any farther into that."

"I think I see part of it. You weren't inexperienced when you came to me. But there was still confusion and hesitancy. It's not all willingness with him, is it?"

"I can't say any more on that; it's complicated."

"That's OK. Just knowing what you're trying to do is enough. I'm going out to Arizona, Rick. I want you to come with me."

"Why?"

"I said it in the photography class you took. I'm making a movie. There's a gay erotica film festival out in a town beyond Phoenix—a town named Mirage. I intend to enter a film and win. I want you there with me."

"Again, why? I don't understand. What do you need me for?"

"The film's already started, Rick. You're the star of the film."

"Me? I don't know anything about acting."

"And that's the glory of it. You're natural and so expressive—and when you take cock, the men watching you want you too. They turn to jelly."

"Shit, man, that's way beyond me. How do you know that?"

"We've already been filming. I've shown scenes around. The men—my clients for the still photography—are going ape over you."

"Already filming?"

"Yes. I'm calling the film *Journey to Mirage*. It's all arty double entendre stuff. It's sure to go over well at the film festival. I've been there before; they eat that stuff up."

"I still don't understand."

"The fantasies, Rick. Your fantasies. You've covered, what, four now, while masturbating? And these are being caught on film. And the locker room scene. Your fantasy was played out. We'll film on the way to Mirage. *Journey to Mirage*. Get it? And we'll make stops along the way and fulfill those fantasies of yours. We only need a couple of more to fill out the film—although it would be nice to have choices and maybe enough for a follow-up film. Each scene will include your fantasy description to me as you masturbate—or I jack you off. And each will be married with a real sex scene that closely evokes the fantasy. Do you understand now?"

A long pause, and then, "I guess so. But I don't know what I think."

"You want to get out of Baltimore, don't you? And you need money. This meets those needs. And there's something else."

"What?" Rick asked.

"You love the fucking. It comes out on film clearly. You may be in some denial on that, but you love it."

"I don't know."

"Yes you do. I'm going to Arizona regardless. If you won't be in the film, I can find someone who will. I've paid you for rights to what's already filmed, though. That leaves you here—without what I've given you in the past few weeks—and with all the pressures that make you want to leave. Think about it. But for only a couple of more days, Rick. I'll be gone before the grass needs to be mowed again."

"I'll . . . I'll think about it."

Groton was working Rick's cock again as this conversation concluded. He leaned over Rick's body once more and took the young man's cock in his mouth. When Rick was groaning and sighing and his hips had involuntarily started to roll, Groton pulled away from the cock and looked up into Rick's face, causing Rick to look down at him.

"I can get up and leave you now, Rick. Is that what you want?"

A short pause and then a quiet, almost strangled "No."

"What is it you want, Rick?"

Another brief silence and then, "You. Inside me. Again."

"That's what I told you, Rick. You do want it. You shy away from it, which is quite endearing for the camera—and I don't want you to lose that sense of vulnerability and innocence—but you do want the cock."

Moving back up Rick's body, Groton moved Rick onto his side and lifted his leg and started the long journey of his cock up into Rick's channel.

Neither said anything for the next twenty minutes, only groaning and grunting and moaning as Groton's embedded cock and Rick's hips moved in a rolling motion—all caught by the clicking and whirring cameras.

"What was that you said?" Rick asked between moans as Groton was working his ass in long, deep strokes.

"Nothing now. Perhaps I'll tell you later."

What Groton had murmured, however, was that Rick's begging for it was all the answer he needed to give Groton on continuing the film and going on the road. All Groton needed to do was deny Rick the cock now to bring him around to acquiescing to the rest.

Chapter Five: Fantasy to Reality

Mr. Crosby, Rick's probation officer, was busily moving papers from one stack to another—and then, seemingly back again—and even took two calls and didn't hurry disconnecting them, as Rick sat across the desk from him and fidgeted. Rick's schedule was tight. He was expected at Groton's house within the hour.

The appointment wasn't to mow the yard this time; they were past that fake excuse stage now. Once there, Rick knew he'd be asked about going on the filming road trip with Groton—and he was afraid Groton would find someone else to go with him before Rick could answer. Rick knew that meant he'd essentially made up his mind about that—or he wouldn't care if Groton had signed on someone else instead. But he was still telling himself he hadn't made up his mind.

And part of Rick's problem in making up his mind was sitting across from him, seemingly ignoring him, even though this was Rick's scheduled time to meet with him.

At last Crosby looked across his desk at Rick, over the top of his eyeglasses, and gave Rick a half smile. "Been keeping yourself clean, Rick?"

"Yes. I never did do any drugs."

"So, you won't care if you're asked to leave a sample on your way out, will you?"

"No, not at all."

"Good. There's a cup on the desk there. You know what to do and where to leave it. And check in before you contribute. You'll need to be watched while you're doing it. You know the drill."

"No problem," Rick said with almost a challenging voice. This wasn't a problem with him. This he could do without hesitation.

"Been keeping clean otherwise? Following all of the requirements of your probation?"

"Yes," given with a far less-challenging tone. "To the extent I can."

"I'm glad you put it that way, Rick. You always must be honest with me. I'm on your side here, you know."

"Yes, I know," Rick said, trying to say that convincingly, knowing it was in his best interests to get on Crosby's good side and stay there as long as possible. Still, he didn't believe for a moment that Crosby was on his side.

"And you know why I said I'm glad you put it that way?"

"Yeah, maybe." Rick hated this dancing around. What did Crosby know?

"Because people see things and tend to report them to us, especially folks who have relatives in the system and want to ease the pressure on them."

"It's not something I can help," Rick said, deciding whether or not Crosby was bluffing, Tony's teasing wasn't something Rick could handle alone anyway. "Sometimes Tony drives by me on purpose—it's not me jumping my probation. I can't stop him doing that."

"I told you I was on your side, Rick. And I am. It helps that you're honest with me. I'll certainly make notes on this that can be used in your favor if conditions warrant. But that isn't all, is it, Rick? There's something else involved here. I've been doing this for a long time, and I sense your problems run deeper than just Tony and his gang."

47

There indeed were deeper issues, but when Rick responded, it was as if he didn't hear that question. And Crosby didn't pursue the point. "What I want—what I think has to happen—is me getting out of town. But I'm stuck here by the courts. You guys say I can't do what I don't really have any control over. You got me in a vice."

"I understand, Rick. I can see how it is."

"But you can't get the probation lifted so I can leave? I've already talked to my mom about her and me going out West somewhere. I don't want to run with any gangs, let alone Tony's. All I want to do is fix cars and keep to myself."

"I understand your position, Rick. But, no, sorry, the probation can't be lifted. But, of course, if I write up the problems you have being here, and you should decide to leave, I'd certainly go to bat for you with the judge if it came to that—as long as you didn't get into any trouble where you went."

Rick looked into Mr. Crosby's eyes, and the probation officer looked back into Rick's eyes with a steady, not unfriendly gaze, and Rick suddenly felt that maybe, just maybe, Mr. Crosby understood after all and really was on his side.

He had been prepared to finger Pete if he had to, but maybe what Tony was doing was enough.

* * * *

"It turns out I don't need you this afternoon, Rick. Something I've been working on has worked out and I need you at about 7:00. I trust you can make it then. It's important."

"Yeah, I guess I can. I can tell my mom I'm going to my friend Eddie's to study for the landscaping class. She'll probably be pleased about that. And she won't be home then anyway. She'll be working a swing evening shift at the hospital."

Rick was thinking as much about not being home alone with Pete as he was with whatever lie he had to spin to be available for Groton. And he was ready to jump at the chance not to be home then.

"What's up for the evening, though?" he asked.

"It's Friday night. Northwestern is playing Patterson at Patterson."

"I don' t understand."

"You will when we get to Northwestern. I'll pick you up at 7:00, down by the corner where I first jacked you off— you don't forget where that is, do you?"

"No," Rick answered, although he wished Groton wasn't so blatant about all of this. And he hadn't actually jacked him off that night. He'd stopped short of that—and thrown Rick all hot and bothered into Pete's arms.

At 7:00 Rick was standing in the designated spot, under the burnt-out street light when Groton rolled up in his old Saab. Spike was in the backseat.

"Get in. In the back with Spike," Groton called across the passenger seat and through the open window.

Spike was dressed in tight football pants and the old-style hip guards again. He was wearing a cut-off T above that, showing off his magnificent ebony abs. He started pawing Rick immediately after the car pulled away from the curb.

"Hey, don't you have nothin' but sex on the brain?" Rick asked as Spike's palm on his basket forced him to spread his legs.

"Nope. But I don't need anything else. With what I got between my legs, I don't need nothin' else. Gotta get in the mood here. Doug says it will save set-up time."

In short order they were pulling up to a rambling group of school buildings and driving around to the back, where Northwestern High School's football field was located. The field—in fact the whole school grounds—appeared to be deserted, although on one side lights were on, shining down on the field and up into the bleachers on that side.

"Everybody out," Groton said cheerily, as he popped the trunk from inside the passenger compartment. "You'll find the same thing Spike's wearing in the trunk, Rick. Change into that, please. And a football. You know how to throw a football, don't you? Bring that out onto the field when you come, please. Spike and the other guys will help me set up the cameras and lights."

The other guys? Still in confusion, Rick asked, "This is Northwestern, according to the sign out front. But what was that about Patterson?"

"Northwestern and Patterson have a big football game tonight," Groton answered in a tone that indicated Rick was being dense, as he turned from where he had already strode toward the field. "That means this field is deserted and available—and everyone from Northwestern who isn't in bed sick is now over at Patterson. I contacted the caretaker here, who has the right needs, and here we are. It was one of your fantasies, Rick. I want to get as much of this film in the can before I start out for Mirage as possible. Now get those football togs on, please. I don't know how much time we can count on out here before we're noticed."

When Rick had changed, he took up the football and walked toward the open gate in the chain-link fence that surrounded the stadium. As he got closer, he saw that there was a tall, meaty Hispanic guy, maybe in his early forties, standing by the open gate and leering at him as he approached.

But Rick looked farther into the field, where he saw Groton and two other guys working with standing floodlights and hand-held video cameras. There had been two other cars parked near where Groton had pulled the Saab up, and Rick now understood that these belonged to the caretaker and the other cameramen.

Spike was standing, looking all black and majestic on about the forty-yard line and a quarter of the way into the side of the field.

"Get as far away from Spike as you feel comfortable, Rick. Then I want you two to throw a few passes to each other. Then, when Spike's ready, I want him to have the ball and you to crouch down into a defensive position. Spike will rush you with the ball and you try to stop him. Spike will take it from there?"

"Spike will take what from there?"

"Your fantasy, Rick. This was your fantasy."

After Spike and Rick had wrestled for the ball a bit on the field, Spike manhandled—more carrying than pushing along—Rick up four rows in the bleachers. He pushed Rick down on his butt on a bleacher seat, with his back arched behind him onto the edge of the next bleacher seat above. Then, Spike, standing on the bleacher foot rail, straddling Rick's knees, ripped open his football pants at the crotch and slowly untied his hip pads. He went down on his knees on the bleacher seat on either side of Rick's thighs, and fed his cock into Rick's mouth, as the cameras clicked and whirred at various angles around him.

After a few minutes of this, Spike was ripping Rick's half T and football pants off and tearing at the laces of Rick's hip pads. Putting his big paws under Rick's thighs, he lifted and spread them, while Rick scrabbled at the wood of the bleacher seats to get whatever purchase he could to hold himself steady—and Spike slowly fed his big, black cock inside Rick's channel and fucked him in fulfillment of the bleacher fantasy Rick had spun out for Douglas Groton a few weeks earlier.

All of this was accompanied by Spike's grunts and Rick's moans and groans and the clicking and whirring of the cameras—and the buzzing of mosquitoes and other critters of the night committing suicide in the floodlights.

When both Rick and Spike had graphically come, Spike left Rick spread-eagled and quivering on the bleachers. Groton and his men took a few last clips of Rick in post-coital dishabille, and then they started breaking down their equipment.

"You're needed over there under that light on the field house behind those goal posts, Rick," Groton said. "Near the open gate."

The lights of the stadium were starting to go off, and as Rick followed Groton down the bleachers to the side of the field, he could see that the caretaker was under the light by the field house and throwing switches on the floodlights.

"Over to that guy?" Rick asked.

"Yes. And take good care of him, Rick. It all happened quickly. We were lucky to be able to set it up. And I agreed to give you to him for a half hour. We'll be waiting in the car."

As Groton and Spike were loading the Saab, the other camera men already having driven off, Rick was going down on his knees in front of the Hispanic caretaker, whose fly was already open with his erect dong out in the air wanting attention. The caretaker buried his fingers in the hair at the back of Rick's head and pulled the young man's face onto his cock.

Groton turned and looked toward the field as he was arranging the cameras in the trunk of the car. He smiled and took a camera back out of the trunk and turned and walked toward the field house. He got there in time to watch the caretaker push Rick down on all fours on the grass under the goal post and mount him from behind. Having only a half hour, he was working faster than Rick could really prepare himself for what was to come.

Later, as they were driving back into Rick's neighborhood in downtown Baltimore, Groton captured Rick's gaze in the rearview mirror and said. "It's time to decide. I want to leave tomorrow. And I want you in bed with me tonight if you're going on this journey. What is it to be, Rick?"

"I'll go," Rick said.

"Good. I'll drop you off and be quick about putting whatever you need in a duffle bag and come back to the drop off place. I wouldn't suggest that you tell that Pete of yours you are going, though. I don't think he wants you to leave Baltimore." Groton chuckled at his own joke.

Rick had already decided he was going. He'd already written and posted a letter to his probation officer saying he was going and why—including the part about Pete. He'd ended by saying the judge could, of course, come after him if he wanted, but that Rick pledged they would all be better off with him out of town. The letter was really to give Crosby some cover. Crosby had been the first—and maybe only—person in this world who had shown any sign of really thinking about what was best for Rick.

* * * *

Later that night, Rick lay on the bed, listening to Groton in the bathroom preparing for the night. As he lay there, he thought about Groton's cock—the longest he'd ever had in him, and wondering if he'd ever taken it all. Spike had managed some depth, but with Spike, it was mostly the stretching of the channel. The Hispanic at the football field had a small cock, but it had had a crook in it that rubbed the head across Rick's prostate, and Rick wasn't sure that the sensation of that wasn't more satisfying than what Spike provided.

But Pete had it all. So, why was Rick running from Pete? Because of his mother, of course. He didn't resent her having a fulfilling sex life. But Pete was fucking her only to get to Rick. Somehow Rick knew that was a fundamental truth. And with Rick gone, that relationship would go one of two ways. Pete would pay complete attention to Maxine, or Pete would leave her. In either case, Rick thought this would be better—more honest—than what was going on now.

Rick grimaced in disgust then, though. What had he become? Comparing the satisfaction of cocks inside him. He'd become a slut. He was addicted. He'd smugly told Crosby he didn't take drugs. But, in reality, he did now. His drug had become the cock. Another man's cock. Any man's cock. He should have been disgusted by the Hispanic caretaker. He wasn't. It had been a little thrilling to know a man—any man—was lost to him like that.

Rick briefly thought about how he could change this, how he could pull away from this behavior. And then he began thinking of what must be ten inches that Groton was carrying—and wondering again if all of it had been inside him. He took the pillows from under his head and moved them to the small of his back, elevating his naked pelvis and spreading his legs wide—wondering if that would provide the angle for him to feel Groton's balls nestled against his crotch, giving purchase for Groton to get it all in him.

The bathroom door opened, and Groton came out and looked at Rick's position and laughed.

"That's very pretty, Rick. But the caretaker taking you made me horny. I liked the image of you being taken like a dog. On the rug please, on all fours."

Groton was unrolling the longest condom Rick had ever seen and rolling it back on his cock, not getting anywhere close to the root with it.

Rick moved off the bed and onto his hands and knees on the carpet. He felt Groton's knees at his hips and Groton's hands on his waist as he hovered over him. Then he felt the bulb at his hole and he held his breath, determined to hold it as long as it took Groton to possess him. But the entry went on forever—for at least three breaths held to their limit. Rick felt what he was consciously waiting, hoping, to feel—the heat of Groton's balls nestled up into his crotch at the edge of the opening to his channel. And then Rick began to groan and pant as, at first, slowly ooooout and iiiiinnn it went to the full length of Groton's ten inches. And then more and more rapidly, and if it could possibly be true, even deeper.

Until, his hand working his own cock, Rick came in two thunderous spurts, his thighs turned to jelly, and, Groton, laughing and still pumping, followed him down, prone on the carpet.

Later, stretched along side each other on the bed, Groton moving his hands over Rick's still-panting body, Groton put his mouth to Rick's ear and whispered, "That was nice. We'll do that again soon. Another fantasy. What else do you fantasize about?"

"I don't think I can say."

"Why not."

Rick thought for a moment, sighing, because Groton's hand had gone to his cock and was beginning to slowly masturbate him.

"I'm afraid."

"You're afraid of your fantasies coming true?"

"Maybe. I guess so. Yes. It's one thing to imagine it— it's quite something else to experience it."

"The intensity of it?"

"Yes. That certainly."

"Think of your most fearful dream, Rick. What is it? Being in a den of lions and tigers?"

"No, I don't think so. Something strange I think. Clowns. Being in a swirl of clowns. Their happy faces turning to sad and then anger. Masked people. Hiding themselves, their true intent."

"Vampires too?"

"Yes, maybe those too."

"You know in some versions vampires are said to have serpent tongues in the heads of their dicks and to have dicks that just keep expanding and expanding inside you. Think of that. And their mouths, when they take your cock in their mouths they suck you all the way down, balls and all, and their tongues piston your cock in rapid motion while they roll your balls in their cheeks. And those tongues in their mouths? Those are like snakes tongues too. You know your piss slit? Those tongues snaking right in there, licking up into the inside of your balls and—"

"Oh . . . god . . . I'm going to come."

"Yes you are," Groton said as he quickly moved his face down to Rick's crotch and swallowed both of his balls into his mouth, moving them to inside his cheeks and rolling them with his tongue as he pumped Rick's cock rapidly to ejaculation with a tight fist.

All the time video cameras at the corners of the ceiling whirred away.

Chapter Six: Blue Ridge Mountains, Virginia

Groton had wanted to get off by 9:30 the next morning, avoiding the worst of the morning rush hours around the Baltimore and Washington, D.C., beltways, but it was closer to 10:30 before the two vehicles got packed with luggage and photographic equipment and nosed into the I-95 traffic south toward Washington.

In addition to Groton, Spike, and Rick, the two cameramen who had helped with the cameras out on the football field were going too. Groton was driving his Saab and he took off with only Spike on board, telling the cameramen where they were to meet late that afternoon and telling Rick to ride with the cameramen because Groton had a couple of more guys to pick up south of Washington. The cameramen, who were introduced to Rick as Phil and Trace, had a Dodge Ram three-quarter-ton quad truck with four doors and half of its truck bed, closest to the back of the cab, outfitted with a covered container where the two men packed away luggage and photographic equipment.

Trace, a big brute probably in his late twenties, was doing most of the heavy lifting, just as Rick had noticed he did the night of the football field shoot. He was the coarser of the two, both in looks and language, and kept giving Rick side looks that left no doubt what he wanted to do. The other guy, Phil, appeared to be the more intelligent and responsible of the two. He was a red head who looked to be in his mid thirties. He was tall and built thinner than Trace was, although when Trace wasn't there for comparison, it was evident he wasn't thin at all. He could probably be described more as sinewy. It looked like he could easily lift whatever needed to be lifted, but that he wasn't as frenetic and mouthy as Trace was and was content to let Trace do any of the grunt work that he was willing to do. And, in contrast to Trace, he looked upon Rick shyly whenever he could be seen to look at him at all.

Trace took the driver's seat, with Phil riding shotgun—which left the backseat of the cab to Rick.

It wasn't more than fifteen minutes before they lost contact with Groton's vehicle. Phil seemed perturbed at this, saying that Trace should be able to keep up with Groton at least past lunchtime, which Groton had mentioned he was having in Culpepper. But Trace just laughed and told Phil that if he didn't like Trace's driving, he should have volunteered to take the wheel. To this, Phil said he had offered to drive and Trace had gruffly stated he was doing it.

Rick was barely able to hear the guys talking in the front seat, not just because of the noise from the truck's powerful Hemi engine but also because they were speaking softly, as if he wasn't there. He just caught snippets of what they were saying, but it mostly was about photographic techniques and equipment.

Traffic was heavy around the Washington Beltway and it was well past noon before they reached the town of Warrenton, some forty-five miles south of the national capital on route 29 and twenty miles short of the planned lunchtime rendezvous in the town of Culpepper.

Trace went off route 29 onto business route 17 and headed into the center of Warrenton.

"What gives?" Phil asked. "We're headed to Culpepper for lunch."

"I'm hungry now. Doug didn't say we had to meet up for lunch; only where he was going to have lunch and split off from us anyway."

"You've just passed up two restaurants," Phil said. They were both speaking loud enough now for Rick to hear, a bit of irritation bubbling up from both. It had been a tough ride through the traffic around the twin big cities.

"Yeah, but I know of a pool hall in the town that has great hamburgers. And I want to relieve the tension of the drive with a game or two of pool."

"We don't have the time."

"Sure we do; we're just going down into Nelson County—and it's for the night."

Phil stopped arguing.

Once in the parking lot, Trace popped out of the cab and sprinted to the tavern door. He was already carrying a hamburger and his first beer over to the pool room before Phil and Rick had entered and figured out the food ordering system there.

Rick was counting his pennies on what he could order when Phil put a hand on his arm—which Rick took notice of, feeling a slight charge of electricity in the connection—and said, "I got yours. Groton told me to pay for you."

They went to a table where they could keep an eye on Trace and try to determine when he was finished with his game of pool and might be convinced to get back on the road.

"Thanks for covering the food," Rick said as they sat down on benches across the table from each other.

"Groton's got you on a tight allowance, has he?"

"He hasn't given me anything toward this trip yet. I've got money of my own, but I don't want to be throwing it around until I know what the deal is on pay."

"Do you have any idea what Groton is piling in on you?"

"What do you mean?"

"It not the art film he's doing for the festival. Any money from that—which isn't guaranteed—won't come for some time. But he's already made a bundle in the still shots and videos he's taken of you completely outside the footage for the film."

"I didn't know that."

"He's already paid Trace and me a couple of thou off the top to travel. You really need to talk to Groton about an advance. You're the talent here."

"The talent?" Rick laughed at the use of that term.

"Of course. I've seen you in action, you know. I know talent when I see it."

Rick looked up into Phil's face and he thought he saw interest there. Rick hadn't thought about the cameramen being turned on by what they were filming. He realized he hadn't thought about a lot of things—other than getting out of Baltimore. But he didn't know if he was brave enough to approach Groton for an advance.

"What is it you want, Rick? What's your goal in life?—I mean what is this film going to get for you? You want to go to California and be a porn star?"

"No, that's not what I want," Rick said, with a nervous laugh. "I guess I haven't thought much beyond getting out of Baltimore. But I do have dreams. I want to work on cars. Maybe in the West, Arizona or New Mexico or some place. I want to fix them. Nothing is more thrilling than hearing a well-tuned engine."

"Nothing?" Phil asked. "Watching you in action indicates you are thrilled by more than that."

Rick laughed nervously again. "I like to be fucked, yes, if that's what you're asking. But I don't see that as a career."

"I'm glad to hear that. I kind of thought that you saw this movie as reality—that Doug had made you see it that way and was using you falsely. It's all a mirage, just like the title, *Journey to Mirage*, says. I think it will make a good movie, but it's not real. There's nothing lasting in it for you."

Rick shrugged and made an exaggerated effort to check on Trace, who was now on his second beer and his second game of pool. Trace was scowling, so Rick decided he must not be winning.

"You know I've been thinking of going out to Arizona too," Phil said, as he laid a hand on Rick's arm to stay Rick from rising out of his seat and going into the pool room. "I want to open a photographic studio of my own. Legitimate stuff—although maybe some gay male glamour shots on the side just to keep life interesting."

"Sounds like a good plan," Rick said, rising in spite of Phil's hand on his arm. He didn't know what Phil was working around to say, but life was complicated enough just now. All the same, his butt was twitching—not necessary just for Phil, but because Groton's encouraging him to have sex fantasies was sending him off into frequent reveries—he had been in heat for days, and, without even thinking about it, he was in the zone of thinking about his next cocking as soon as his last one had ended. He'd been having images of being bound and taken as they were driving down through northern Virginia, and he was still keyed up by that—and finding that it was an arousing concept. He'd never really thought of that before. Thanks to Groton, he was fantasizing almost constantly these days.

They didn't have to pull Trace away from the table, though, he'd run the balls on his last game and was happy now and had downed his beer and was coming out of the men's room and telling them it was time to shove off.

When they got to the truck, he turned to Phil and gruffly said, "You drive now. I want to sit in back with Rick for a while."

"I don't think that's a good idea, Trace," Phil said. "Groton said . . . I know what you said when you heard the kid was riding with us, but Groton would flail you alive if—"

But Trace was already shoving Rick up onto the backseat of the Ram and was climbing in behind him. "You're the one who wants to make tracks and meet a schedule. Stop standin' here and jawing about it, and let's get rolling."

Phil turned around in the seat and spoke directly to Rick. "You can come up here, Rick, if you want. You don't have to stay back there."

"It's OK. I'm OK here," Rick answered in a small voice. He knew what was happening, and Trace wouldn't be his first choice—even against Phil—but it was becoming an addiction for Rick. His own dick was already straining at his jeans pouch. The very musky aroma of a horny man was a stimulant to his libido—and there was no doubt that Trace was horny.

Trace's bulk was taking up a lot of the room in the back of the cab, and he had an arm around Rick and holding him close before they were out of the parking lot.

Before they were back out on 29, Trace was feeling Rick up good and could tell from Rick's heavy breathing and the feel of his cock through the material of his blue jeans that Rick was going to let him have his way. Trace moved his hands under the material of Rick's armless T—the hand of the embracing arm snaking through the deep arm slit, with a thumb and forefinger going to one of Rick's nipples, making him flinch and moan. The other hand went, first, to Rick's trembling belly and then down, brushing across his basket, and then back up to the zipper pull of Rick's jeans.

"What's that?" Rick asked with a hoarse voice, writhing already at the action of Trace's hand on his freed cock, as Trace pulled him over onto his lap and extracted a black rubbery device out of his pocket that was a good six inches long and bulbed out in oblong protrusions at either end.

"This? This is a blackjack. Never seen one before? It comes in handy for when I go clubbing in rough parts of town at night. And these are just leather strips. Ever done it bound before?"

"No," Rick said in a breathy voice.

"Ever thought of it?"

"Yeah. But just for the first time earlier today."

"First. I wanna fuck you. I'm horny as hell, and you feel like you are too. Any objections to that? You do it for anyone Groton points to, so I think you can do it for me."

A pause, as Trace moved the blackjack under the hem of Rick's T and slid it up to his chest and started playing with his nipples with it?

"No, I guess not." And then. "No, not at all. Hurry please."

"So, wanna try it bound?"

"Yes, yes, anything. Just don't make me wait too long." Rick was trying not to whine, but he wasn't having much success at it.

"Now ain't that nice," Trace muttered. "Our pretty boy's a nympho."

A warning word of "Trace" was called out from the front seat, but Trace just ignored Phil, and Rick was too far gone to do more than groan and repeat, "Hurry, please hurry."

Rick watched in fascination as Trace pulled his T over his head and bound his wrists together. And, unexpectedly, Trace raised Rick's arms and lodged the bound wrists behind his neck, causing Rick to arch his chest toward the back of the front seat. Rick could feel Trace's cock engorged underneath him, and he was more than ready for the fuck. Occasionally he'd look into the rearview mirror and could see Phil looking back at them, a worried expression on his face. But he had his hands full keeping the truck on the road headed south.

"OK, pretty boy. I want more time. But I'll give you something to think about while you're waiting for Joe—I call it Joe—to fill the darkness."

Trace pulled Rick's jeans and briefs off his legs and then raised up and stripped his off as well. He moved Rick's butt up and into his belly. This put Rick's cock more or less on top of Trace's. With one hand, Trace encased both cocks and began a slow jack off, while he moved the blackjack around Rick's arched chest and his belly and thighs with the other hand, gliding on flesh and making little flicks of rubber on delicate skin.

When Rick ejaculated, unable to keep himself from going over the top quickly, he expected Trace to move his cock to his ass canal and start fucking him—to give him relief there—but again Trace surprised him.

"Find someplace private to pull off. Where we won't be seen," Trace called out to Phil.

"Trace, no. If Groton finds out—"

"Groton won't find out unless you or pretty boy here tells him. You want to be fucked by a real man now, pretty boy?"

"Yes. Oh, god, yes," Rick moaned.

"You heard him. He wants it. He wants it bad. So, pull over, Phil."

Phil, as demanded, found a spot behind a stand of bushes down a driveway to a house with boarded up windows that obviously was deserted. Then he sat deeply in the driver's seat, staring straight ahead, obviously pretending he wasn't even there.

Without untying Rick's wrists, Trace manhandled him out of the cab and back to the rear of the truck, where he let down the tailgate and laid down a tarp for Rick to lay his back on. Then he raised Rick's arms over his head and hooked his wrist bonds on a hook at the side of the container wedged in back of the cab and pushed the young man's ankles through plastic hoops that were dangling from the back corners of the bed on either side.

Thus bound, Trace opened the container and took out a duffle bag and forced it under the small of Rick's back so his ass was presented to Trace, while Rick moaned and groaned for the exotic fuck. Trace didn't start fucking him immediately, though, he used the blackjack as an enticer on Rick's bare skin for a while and then as a dildo for a while, and Rick was begging for the cock—not caring whose it was—before Trace gave it to him.

First the handle end of the blackjack and then the bulbier oval of the business end, covered with Trace's spit and worked slowly in as Rick panted and strained at his bonds. Rick was finding he loved the sensation of having no control, being forced, bound. This was the balance that contributed fully to his arousal and satisfaction, taking the guilt away. All responsibility was taken off him for doing what he knew wasn't right, that was telling about his base needs and desires, and at the same time he no longer had any control over it, was a prisoner to the wants and urges of the other man. The pleasure of it was freeing and excruciating for Rick, and when the blackjack was gone, replaced by Trace up on the tailgate on his knees, lifting Rick's pelvis to him with hands cupping, squeezing, and separating Rick's butt cheeks, the preparation of the blackjack aided Trace's cruel plunge into the quick of him, and as Trace began churning away inside him, he was not even looking at Trace, not caring who it was as long as he had a dick inside him. Rick strained in delightful ineffectiveness against his bonds, arched his back, let his eyes roll to the waving branches of trees above his head, concentrated on fantasizing a big, black bruiser—Pete—between his thighs, wailed his total satisfaction—and ejaculated a second time.

With a humming Trace behind the wheel again, they drove the rest of the way down 29 and over toward the foothills of the Blue Ridge with no more than the tersest comments between Phil and Trace and with Rick lying along the backseat of the cab and moaning.

* * * *

At Charlottesville, the RAM turned toward the mountains and then, just before the start of the incline up to the pass over the Blue Ridge at Afton, they turned south into a valley. They were driving into Virginia's Nelson County now. They proceeded for a couple of miles and then turned back toward the mountains and pulled up into a graveled parking lot at a rambling log roadhouse with a neon sign in red over it that said "Lefty's" inside a heart shape.

To the surprise of neither Phil nor Trace, Groton had already arrived. He was standing out at the end of the walk up to the door of the roadhouse talking with a monster of a man in brown trousers with suspenders over a red flannel shirt. Spike was standing several yards away from the two, staring up at an upper window of the roadhouse, where a shirtless black-headed guy with good musculature was staring back down at him, framed by the molding on the window. Spike may or may not have been listening to the conversation between the other two men, because he was gazing pretty intently at the man in the window. Behind the monster man, close in his shadow, his arm under the grip of the big man, was a young blond guy, barefoot, and in just low-slung jeans, shyly looking at the ground.

Lounging at the door of the roadhouse were two buxom bottle blondes in tight-fitting blouses and shorts.

And leaning against Groton's Saab that Trace parked beside were two lanky and slightly mean and unclean looking country boys with bad teeth, who leered at Rick as he struggled with some effort out of the backseat of the RAM well after Trace and Phil had descended and were walking toward Groton. The two guys at the Saab leaned in to each other and were talking quietly as they eyed Rick and laughed.

Groton looked appraisingly at Rick as he slowly walked up to the gathered group. Although he was looking at Rick, when he spoke, it was to the monster man. "See what I mean? Isn't the resemblance uncanny?"

"Yes, I do see it," the man spoke on a rich bass voice. "Course ones blonder than the other. This must be Rick, your film's star. He's dynamite. Where did you ever find him?"

"He found me, you could say. But I'm bringing him along. Rick, come over and meet my old friend Lefty Drake. He's going to help us with some of the filming."

Then he turned to Phil and Trace and said, "You two can go on in. The girls will show you where your rooms are. The rooms are pretty utilitarian and small, but they serve their purpose—and will serve ours too. We'll just be here for a few days. Oh, and I'd like to talk to you both separately this evening, please." The last sentence was spoken somewhat ominously. Phil winced, but Trace just smiled a sloppy smile.

As they went back to the truck for their bags and joined the buxom blondes at the front door of the roadhouse, Spike touched Groton's arm and said, "I'll go in too and they can show me where I'm bunking too."

"Yeah, go ahead," Groton said, but Spike wasn't looking at him now, he was looking up to the window where the shirtless young man, his chest covered with curly black hair, was still smiling down at those below—or rather at Spike himself.

"You should meet Billy Dan, too," Groton turned and said to Rick. "I've just met him myself, but I thought maybe I was meeting you again. The two of you are the spitting image of each other."

Lefty pulled the young blond guy out from his shadow and into the light. "Say hi to Rick, Billy Dan," Lefty said.

Billy Dan looked up but only briefly and gave Rick a shy smile and a quiet, "Glad to meet ya," before returning his gaze to his toes, which he was curling and uncurling in the grass beside the walk.

Rick gave him a brief "Hello," while he looked for where the others were seeing the resemblance. But he, like most folks, wasn't really able to see himself in others.

"He's certainly acting virginal enough," Groton said to Lefty and then laughed. "Sure he's unused?"

"Yep, he's willing enough—says he needs the money to get out of Nelson County but also that he's that way inclined—but I've been saving him for something special. Maybe you and I can get him started."

"Yeah, maybe," Groton answered and laughed. "And maybe you and me—and him—can talk about some possibilities later."

"Well, come on in," Lefty said. "I got private rooms at the back. I'll let the front take care of itself tonight. Business should start up as soon as it gets dark. You can leave your cars out here, if you want. Most of the clients park in back of the building, though." He laughed a hearty laugh then and put one arm over Groton's shoulder and turned him toward the door to the roadhouse and took Billy Dan's arm in a firm grip with the other. As they stepped off on the walk, he looked around and gave Rick a welcoming—and frankly assessing—look.

Rick started to follow, but at the sound of a familiar noise—a human groan—he looked up at the window the shirtless guy had been smiling down from to see that the young man no longer alone. He was now leaning half out of the window, his fists gripping the wood of the frame hard. His face showed a mixed expression of pain and ecstasy, which Rick had no trouble figuring out, because Spike's big black paws were covering his nipples, Spike's chin was hooked on the young man's shoulder, and the guy's torso was swaying back and forth in the unquestionable movement of the fuck from the rear.

As Rick entered the reception room of the roadhouse, a bunch of both young women and men were sitting about in various versions of provocative dress. He needed no more evidence to conclude what this roadhouse dealt in.

If Rick hadn't figured it out before, he would have known when he was led to a bedroom—which was more the size of a cell—where only a limited attempt at decoration had been made. It was quite functional for the purpose it usually was being used for—and it did have a window, which was right next to the one where he'd seen the shirtless guy, Rick figured from the sound of fucking going on in the room next to him. The shirtless guy was quite vocal. And, as Rick well knew, Spike could pull loud sounds of taking out of a man.

The door had been open to the room at the other side of his when Rick was shown upstairs and he could see that it was larger and had a king-sized bed in it and a lot of red velour trappings around. He had thought it no doubt was the establishment's deluxe suite.

He wasn't surprised to find out that Groton was assigned to it. The walls of this room were no thicker than the one on the other side, though, Rick discovered later that night. The special occasion that Lefty had been saving Billy Dan for turned out to be to share him for his first taking with Groton. The headboard of the king-sized brass bed was against the wall Rick's bed was set lengthwise against, and Rick's own bed was rocked for nearly two hours in the night by the rhythmic pounding of the headboard on his wall accompanied by the unmistakable sound of Billy Dan's first taking. First by Groton, as the guest, and then, at greater length and more vocalization from Billy Dan by Lefty.

That racket had barely toned down to a plaintive moaning by Billy Dan when Rick's own door opened and a heavy body came down on top of him. Rick was lying on his belly, and Spike covered his body with his, writhing around on Rick's back and nipping at his ears and the hollow neck with his teeth, until Rick began panting and, with effort, raised his hips in presentation to the familiarity of Spike's channel-spitting cock.

"Where are the cameras?" Rick murmured between groans of the invasion of Spike's cock.

"It don't need to be acting a scene for me to want to be inside you," Spike muttered.

"The same with me," Rick whispered.

"But can't let Doug know that," Spike said. "That Groton's a jealous bastard. You shouda' heard him reaming Phil and Trace this evening."

Just then they heard someone in the hallway, and Spike barely was able to move to the back of where the door would open when it did open and Groton was standing in the hall, stark naked.

"The rest of the night in my bed with me, if you please, Rick."

Rick got up and moved through the door and was guided back into the room beside him.

Lefty was fucking a dazed and groaning Billy Dan on the bed again—or still. The young blond was on his back, his butt at the edge of the side of the bed, his legs spread wide, a stack of pillows under the small of his back, his torso arched back, and his head lolling to the side in near unconsciousness.

Lefty was a big, rough, hairy beast with heavy cock and balls to match. He wasn't wearing a condom—no doubt with the understanding that Billy Dan was no physical threat on his first taking—which Rick could tell because Lefty was bringing his cock all the way out before slamming it back into Billy Dan's channel. Billy Dan's body was twitching with each plunge. The cum of several fuckings, not all Lefty's, no doubt, was dribbling out of his channel and down the side of the sheeted mattress.

Groton pulled Rick around to the other side of the bed and laid him down in a mirror image to Billy Dan's, spread his legs, and plunged his own long, thin cock inside Rick's channel. Rick turned his face to Billy Dan's and they eyed each other as each was being taken.

Billy Dan looked so beleaguered yet determined to get beyond the threshold, that Rick gave him a concerned look and reached over with a hand and cupped the other young man's cheek with the palm of his hand in comfort. He wanted to tell Billy Dan that the first time didn't have to be like this. It could be gentle and loving and patient—and not in surroundings like this. But then he checked himself. His first time hadn't been any of those things. Tony had just pushed him through the rear passenger door and down on his belly on the backseat of a car they were chopping, held his arm against his back and bent up almost to the point of breaking it, jerked down Rick's shorts and briefs, and fucked him hard as Rick screamed his head off for mercy and patience that didn't come in echoes reverberating around the cavernous warehouse. Then he had turned him on his back, with Rick's feet scrambling for purchase on the roof of the car chassis and against the frame of its driver's door, had fucked him a second time.

Still, Rick believed it didn't have to be this way. And not just the first time, either. Each time.

Billy Dan turned his lips to Rick's palm as if in thanks for the attempt at comfort through this ordeal. And, instinctively, Rick moved his lips to Billy Dan's and they kissed to find some affection in the situation as Lefty and Groton churned away between their respective pairs of thighs on opposite sides of the bed.

When Lefty had come, he turned the limp body of Billy Dan so that it was laying on one side of the bed naturally and left the room, turning off the light as he left.

Groton fucked on. He could go at it for long stretches of time and then be ready to go again after a short break for recharging. When he was finished, he climbed over Rick, stretched out in the middle of the bed beside the still-moaning Billy Dan and pulled Rick in full length between him and the other side of the bed.

Rick hadn't come yet, and Groton held him in a tight embrace with one hand and started stroking his cock with the other.

"A fantasy. Give us a fantasy."

Rick was half asleep and wasn't even thinking much about what he was saying. "Bound. I'm bound, my arms above my head, my legs spread wide."

"Bound, eh. Where. Where are you bound."

"A tailgate. The tailgate of a truck."

Groton stopped stroking and held Rick so tightly he hardly could breathe. "So it was Trace, then. That's his specialty. I was going to make you tell me who fucked you this afternoon. But now I don't have to—or was it both of them? Tell me."

"No, neither of—"

"Don't lie to me, Rick. Don't ever lie to me."

Rick yelped in pain, as Groton had gripped both of his balls in a fist and squeezed hard. He maintained the vice grip, with Rick's eyes immediately beginning to water and his body going stiff as a board.

"It was Trace. Just Trace. Phil tried to stop it . . . but I wanted it."

"Did you beg for it, or did he make you want it by what he did to you?"

"I wanted it—but it didn't have to be from him. Oh, god, let up, Mr. Groton. I can't stand it. Yes, yes, he would have taken it even if I didn't want it. That's what Phil was on him about."

The grip loosened, and Rick let out an involuntary whimper.

To his shame, Rick wanted it again. He wanted Groton to jerk him off as he tried to come up with another fantasy and then to fuck him again. But, perhaps as punishment, Groton released his hold on Rick and rolled over and turned Billy Dan on his side, cuddled into his body, and Rick heard the exhausted groan and little cry as Groton began running his cock back up into Billy Dan's channel and beginning the rhythm of a fuck that made the mattress move under Rick's body like he was on the ocean.

Rick was nearly asleep when Groton turned back to him and started taking him in the same position he'd just taken Billy Dan.

This rotation, punctuated by brief bouts of dozing, went on for most of the rest of the night.

Near dawn, Groton was holding Rick close again and stroking his cock, which brought Rick slowly back toward consciousness.

"A fantasy. Tell me another fantasy, Rick." Rick looked around and saw that Groton had set up two video cameras on stands that were panned on the bed. Rick understood that it was show time again.

This brought a scenario to Rick's mind. It may have occurred because of what he had been thinking earlier about it not having to be this way—or more likely because of the new experience the previous afternoon with Trace of the bindings, and, specifically, the lack of control and choice at the height of the act. But what came to mind wasn't so much a fantasy as a reality that Rick had tried to bury deep inside him but that surfaced sometimes when he had brought himself to degradation—being taken hard and without choice or control . . . and wanting it. Like with Trace that afternoon at the back of the truck. He knew he was whoring, but he had wanted it so bad. And he had wanted it even though he knew that Phil disapproved—although Rick didn't know why he cared what Phil thought about it. Phil was someone he'd only really talked to once—and had barely touched, even though the touch was electric. For some reason he did care what Phil thought, however.

As Groton stroked Rick's cock and cajoled him to weave a fantasy as fingers of light began to invade the window of the now-quiet roadhouse bordello, Rick almost began to speak. The words were on his lips. "I'm alone in a prison cell with a hulking black man with muscles, a huge dick, and an attitude." But he held off; he couldn't do it. He knew the film was about fantasy turned into reality. But Rick had already lived the reality of this.

Taken from the chop shop by the police as the only one who didn't escape. Interrogated, but not giving Tony and his crew up—to the point of irritating the policemen who intentionally put him in a holding cell with a gang member from an all-black gang that was a bitter rival of Tony's gang. The police figuring that Rick was a member of Tony's gang, so why not let a rival gang member help loosen his tongue and resolve. A gorilla of a black ganger, all muscle and tattoos, and cock, and attitude. Getting the wink from the guard who tossed Rick into the cell with him. Having his heavy dick out and forcing it into Rick's mouth almost before the guard had clanged the cell door shut. Then Rick hanging onto the bars of the cage cell with dear might, and screaming for help and relief that never materialized, as the black monster pulled his hips away from the bars with a firm grip and banged his cock again and again and again, relentlessly, up into Rick's channel until he himself was worn out and flopped down on his back on the lower bunk, slung his arm over his eyes, and snored himself to sleep.

Rick slumping, moaning, to the ground inside the bars of the cage until the interrogators returned and, not having gotten any more cooperation—with most of what they were asking being far beyond anything Tony had let Rick know anyway—deciding to leave Rick in the cage with the black ganger all night.

Then the first shame for Rick—what he just could not tell as a fantasy to Groton and then have to live all over again in a reality phase. Rick dragging himself over to the bunk. Wanting it again. Climbing on top of the black ganger and, to the willing amusement of the monster, straddling those meaty hips and guiding the plump, reengorging cock into position, and fucking himself on that big black cock again. Because he wanted it. Because he couldn't help himself from wanting it again. And before dawn begging for it a third time.

And then, the recurring shame thereafter. Whenever Pete was fucking him, reliving the barred cage experience—and letting it arouse himself all the more, and because he responded so wildly, so fully, Pete wanting more of it too. A vicious circle of want and degradation.

No, Rick could not bring himself to reveal this fantasy to Groton. So he feigned groggy sleepiness, and willed his cock to go flaccid under Groton's ministrations. Which, thankfully it did—at least enough for Groton to lose interest in hearing another fantasy he could develop for his film.

When Rick woke, it was well into the next morning and he was alone in Groton's bed.

Chapter Seven: The Meadow

When Rick came downstairs into the room that served as a dining room and staff lounge when it wasn't the main club room, he found only Phil from those of Groton's crew, sitting there and sipping on coffee and looking generally morose. A few other women and men Rick now knew were part of Lefty's establishment and rented by the half hour, were scattered about other tables, all in various forms of undress, the women keeping to themselves and the men the same. On the whole the women looked well used and a bit scraggly and the men looked more fit. Rick wondered if guys were less picky with the women they fucked than the men they'd fuck. The pair of staring guys Groton and Spike had stopped to pick up on their way here were sitting at a table in the corner by themselves. As soon as Rick came down the stairs, they turned their attention to him with licentious, hooded gazes, as they licked lips, flashed yellow- and blackened-tooth smiles, and held a private little conversation between themselves.

The only one moving around was Billy Dan, who was serving as waiter, taking coffee from table to table and looking cheerful despite a certain pained delicateness in his walk. He bestowed a shy smile on Rick as Rick hit the bottom step of the stairs and, signaling with the coffee carafe, put the question of whether Rick wanted a cup. Rick did and he smiled back with his return signal.

Rick was relieved to find Billy Dan here and in good spirits. That erased most of the guilt of doing nothing when he was being initiated into male sex the previous night. Obviously Lefty had been right about Billy Dan wanting it and just needing to get started.

As Billy Dan was pouring Rick a cup of coffee and giving him a "we have intimately shared, so we are brothers" look, Rick gave the cameraman who had shown some concern for Rick, Phil, a questioning look and was invited to sit down beside him. They both turned and watched Spike come down the stairs, his arm around the dark, shirtless—and still shirtless—man in the window from the previous day, and the two sat down at a table to themselves, lost in each other like no one else was in the room. Rick had little doubt where Spike had gone after the near miss of Groton finding him in Rick's room—the room Rick had started out in—the previous night. What Rick wondered, though, was what had motivated Spike to interrupt his coupling with the shirtless guy to come to Rick's room.

Rick turned from that couple, wondering if Spike had gone off him now, at least for couplings outside of the film—and not being sure he liked that. He rather wanted to know what he and Spike could do together when it was spontaneous and not for the cameras. To stifle that thought, he opened the conversation with Phil.

"You're looking a little sad this morning, Phil. A bad night?"

"You could say more reserved and guarded than sad."

"Where's Trace? Has he already had breakfast, or is he maybe still up in the rooms with one of Lefty's men?"

"He's gone. Groton rather loudly gave him the heave ho earlier this morning. Groton's gone over to Charlottesville—and on to Richmond, if necessary—to try to find a replacement camera jockey by this afternoon."

"Oh? What happened?"

"I think you know what happened. You told Groton what Trace did with you. I thought we made it pretty clear that Groton wouldn't like that one bit."

"I'm sorry, Phil. Yeah, I told Groton about it—but he knew it already and he forced me to. I did it mainly because he was talking like both of you had been in on it, and I had to make it clear that you weren't."

"Thanks for that. I need this job."

They sat there in silence for a few minutes, sipping on their coffee, not looking at each other.

"Anyway, I'm glad Groton found out about it and gave Trace the gate. Trace and I have worked together off and on for years, but he can be a real crude mother fucker."

"Listen, I know you don't approve. I can tell it by how you—"

But Phil broke in. "Let's not talk about this here. There are picnic tables out back, by the creek that runs behind this dump. Let's refresh our coffee and go out there."

Rick's sensations soared. Getting Phil alone was arousing to him. For some reason he couldn't identify, he was gravitating toward Phil.

When they were sitting side by side on a table, their feet on a bench, facing the tumbling creek and their backs to the world of Groton and Lefty, Phil was the first to speak.

"You sure this is what you want to be doing, Rick?"

"You really don't approve, do you? You can't see how I'm at a place where the sex is good—that I just want to let loose. That doesn't mean I'll be like that forever."

"I understand, but—"

"Trace didn't rape me, you know. I wanted it then. But I've got to say—"

"I know. I'm trying not to judge. I just think you're worth more than that. That the act should have more meaning. This way can steal your senses and, in time, can make it all meaningless. It can numb you to the good things that can come from making love with someone you actually love. And you're doing it for money that Groton hasn't given you. At least that's what I think, what I believe."

"It's just something that's come over me all of a sudden and is sort of overwhelming. I don't mean for this to be forever. I have other things I want to do. And Groton did give me some money. I asked him again last night and he gave me some."

"How much?"

"A couple of hundred bucks."

Phil sighed a deep sigh. "Chickenfeed," he finally said.

There was a short pause while both concentrated on the foaming, racing water in the creek and avoided looking at each other.

"And what I was going to say when you interrupted," Rick said, returning to safer conversational ground, "was that the one thing I wished yesterday was . . . was that it had been you rather than Trace."

"Me too," Phil mumbled.

"What did you say?" Rick said, as if he hadn't heard Phil.

Phil turned his face toward Rick and started to speak again, to repeat what he'd said. But Rick took the opportunity to take Phil's lips in his before Phil could speak.

They kissed, deeply, hungrily. But then Phil pulled away as Rick was putting his hands on him.

"We can't. You know what happened to Trace. I need the job . . . and, more to the point, I'm not going to do it easy. I want it, but I can't do it when you're like this. It means more to me than a toss in the hay."

"I think it could mean more to me too . . . with you, Phil."

They were interrupted by the sound and sight of a Saab rounding the curve in front of the roadhouse. The car roared on. It wasn't Groton, but they both knew that it could have been. Phil quickly rose from the picnic table and put some distance between him and Rick. And Rick, fully appreciating the danger Phil had spoken of, didn't try to stop him. But, as Phil started to walk back to the roadhouse, Rick did stop him by posing a question.

"You said Groton was trying to find a cameraman for this afternoon."

Phil turned to face Rick. "Yeah, we're here because we're filming another one of your fantasy scenes today. Groton didn't tell you?"

"No. What . . . scene?"

"If you don't know, then I'm not the one to ask," Phil said almost gruffly. "These are your fantasies, not mine. Your choices, not mine. I just hold a camera. And I don't go in for anything as wild as we've already shot."

And then he turned and strode back around the corner of the roadhouse, making Rick feel diminished as he sat on the picnic table. His hand went to his lips, where Phil had been, if ever so briefly. And he trembled and felt a sense of regret.

* * * *

Phil and the new cameraman, a guy named Roger, who kept taking furtive glances at Rick with a "caught with a hand in the cookie jar" expression on his face as they went along, were in the front seat of the Dodge RAM and Rick in the back as they left the roadhouse and drove further up in a cut back between one mountain and another. They were following Groton's Saab, occupied by Groton, Spike, and the two staring hillbillies Groton had picked up the previous day. Between the Saab and the truck cruised an old Cadillac Seville, driven by Lefty and with four other guys from the roadhouse inside.

They reached a turnoff that went up hill toward an old farmhouse and a meadow covering the rise of a hillock, and Phil stopped the Dodge as the two other cars proceeded to the farmhouse.

"Why have we stopped here?" Rick asked.

"If you don't know, don't ask me," Phil answered. "Like I said this morning, it's your fantasy. I just know we're to wait here ten minutes and then drive up there behind that old tumbling-down barn. Roger here, and I, are to get our gear together. I'm to go out in the meadow and Roger into the house and you're to wait in the truck for ten minutes after that and then go up and knock on the door to the house. Ring any bells, does it?"

Rick shuddered and shrank into the seat because it did, indeed, ring bells in his head.

It was fifteen minutes alone in the truck in advance of his appointed time before Rick virtually stumbled out and slowly dragged himself toward the door of the old farmhouse. He was trembling with anticipation. In doing so, his emotions were mixed. If this had come before he and Phil had talked at the picnic table that morning, he would have walked swiftly, ass twitching in anticipation, although still a little fearful at the magnitude of what the playing out of the fantasy could entail—the multiplicity of men that this fantasy had evoked. But now, he had reservations.

If only his conversation with Phil had not made him think.

Groton was standing near the door, the camera pointed at Rick as he crossed the hardscrabble yard toward the old house. Rick tried to calm himself, steeling himself to play for the camera, searching his mind for how he should be acting like not knowing what he was to find when that door opened to him—but not being able to force what he knew he would find out of his mind.

Lefty opened the door to his knock. He was naked, as were the other men in the room, in various stages of high suck. In contrast to most of the thin and stringy men in the room, Lefty was a veritable bear, a monster of a man, with a slight paunch and low hanging and heavy balls and cock. The new cameraman, Roger, was at the other side of the room. He had been panning the orgy in what had been the house's living room, but the camera had come up, focused on the door to get Rick's expression, when Lefty opened the door to him.

The sight of Lefty alone, the leer on his face if nothing else, brought out the expression the camera desired from Rick even though the element of surprise was incomplete. Rick was so expressive that those seeing the film would never know it wasn't a complete surprise.

Lefty put out a hand to take Rick's arm and pull him into the room, but the gesture was feigned. If he wanted Rick in the room, he would easily have been able to effect that. But the fantasy was the fantasy and must be the reality of the moment, and Rick turned and ran for the meadow.

Most of the mountain men were in their element and were fleet of foot on this terrain, even barefooted. Lefty and Spike and the two cameramen at the house, Groton and Roger, all could have easily been outdistanced by Rick, if that was what he was trying to do.

But the other five men—the two Groton had driven in to the roadhouse with the previous day and the three Lefty had brought into the hidden hollow in the mountains from the roadhouse that afternoon—were faster than Rick. And they had been well versed in what to do. They were all salivating at the roles they were to play.

Phil, at the far end of the meadow, filmed the action as Rick ran toward him and was caught in the trap of a circle of leering, taunting, naked men. Groton and Roger were filming from behind.

The circle tightened, and the men began to reach out for Rick, to turn him in circles. Their bare feet caught Rick at the ankles and made him tumble.

He rose and lunged to one side, trying seemingly desperately to break through the circle. But strong, sinewy hands, backed up a lusty laugh, clutched him and spun him back into the circle and to his knees. He rose again, and turned in a circle, looking for an opening or the weakest link. But there was no weakness there in the men of the mountains. They were all nimble and determined and working in consort.

A foot flashed out, Rick went down again—this time to stay down, as the circle had closed in upon him and five pair of hands were tearing at his clothing, rendering him as naked as the mountain men were.

What flashed through his mind was the image of his clothes being rendered unusable after this was over. But this was just a movie. There was nothing sinister to anticipate from that. Was there? Groton will have brought something else for Rick to put on. Wouldn't he? For the first time, doubt crept into Rick's mind on where this movie was headed.

He had one—and then two—cocks pressing at his lips and strong hands clutching his hips and the bulb of a hard cock at his channel as Spike and Lefty reached the circle.

"Smallest to largest. It looks like Lefty last—right after me," Spike called out as he reached down into the swarming pile and pulled a body off Rick's. "You don't really want to claim smallest, do you?"

Rick moaned.

Then the fucking began, while Rick was moved from belly to back and to belly again, as a succession of progressively larger cocks slid inside him and cameras whirred from three directions. After the third cock, Rick was numb from the waist down and felt little—until Lefty moved between his legs. Rick cried out and arched his back, panting and gasping, fighting for breath and scrabbling his hands out ineffectually in search for stability, as Lefty pulled him up into the air with strong hands on his hips, rolling him up on his shoulder blades. And began fucking down into his now-gaping hole with a monster cock.

Rick thought he had endured it all when he felt Lefty shudder and come, but over the ringing in his ears, he heard Groton chime out, "For the finale, what's bigger than Lefty?"

And almost immediately, Rick found out. Lefty lifted him, and was putting him down on his back, which Rick discovered wasn't going to be on the grass of the meadow. There was a body stretched under his, its cock in full erection.

Rick's channel was lowered on this cock—which belonged to one of the staring hillbillies Groton had brought in the previous day.

As Rick groaned and almost hyperventilated, he watched the approach of the other hillbilly between his legs.

And then Rick was being double worked by two cocks at once. These men must have done this before. They knew just how to keep both cocks inside his channel with at least one of them stroking at a time.

All the time, three cameramen moved around him in an intricate dance of "catch it all" as the film whirred away.

* * * *

Latter, in the night, lying there in Groton's bed in the roadhouse, his channel throbbing from the multiple fuckings it had taken—but also swept by a feeling of awe and waves of arousal that he did, in fact, take it and revel in it despite the fright of it all—Rick lay perfectly still, feigning sleep. He wasn't so recovered that he wanted Groton at him tonight. He was exhausted and needed to rest—and needed the throbbing inside his channel to recede.

But Groton wasn't bothering Rick—at least not yet. As the night before, Groton was in the middle, with Rick on one side and Billy Dan on the other.

Groton was turned toward Billy Dan and embracing him, one hand slowly working the young man's cock.

"Tell me a fantasy, Billy. I know you have dreamed of exotic takings. Spin me a tale. It will help you come more satisfactorily."

"Exotic?" Billy Dan whispered back. Was it possible he'd never heard a word like that before? Had Billy Dan ever been out of the foothills of the Blue Ridge, Rick wondered? Would he have any idea what might lay ahead of him? How easily he might be taken advantage of and degraded?

Rick almost laughed out loud at this thought. Where had he come from if not a backwoods of his own—an ethnic urban ghetto? And how open had his mind been before he began spiraling down to where he was today?

But at least Rick had been disposed to it—without knowing it until Tony had forced him. But he'd quickly discovered that he liked it, wanted it, was even seeking it out now. Was Billy Dan blessed with that propensity too, or did he have a tough road ahead of him?

"Special, unusual, that's what exotic is," Groton murmured patiently. "Something that you might be ashamed for others to know makes you feel sexy. Although here, like this, you should not feel reluctant to tell me anything. You are laying with a man, who is working your cock, and, after you have come, is going to fuck you."

Rick heard Billy Dan's deep moan at having that spoken.

"A man who has already fucked you in many ways," Groton continued. "There is nothing you can't tell me about how you have fantasized about being fucked by a man. Relax, as I stroke you, and tell me of how you have imagined being taken in an unusual way."

Don't do it, Rick screamed in his mind. At first, since there was no sound from the other side of the bed for a moment other than Billy Dan's deep groaning, Rick was afraid he'd said it out loud. But he hadn't. His concern was no less, though, in wanting Billy Dan to stop and think hard before he went down that road with Groton. It had only been a mental exercise of Rick's to want to be gang banged—being doubled was beyond his imagination at the time he had spun that fantasy for Groton. Having experienced it now, Rick understood that reality far outstripped curiosity. But if he was honest with himself, he had never risen to the heights of arousal and the feeling of being completely taken as during what he had done this afternoon.

But why should he feel so concerned for Billy Dan? Was this some complication Phil had imposed on him—not speaking of his disapproval of this behavior but asking questions of Rick that he didn't want to face?

That was when Rick's eyes went up to the ceiling—to the corners of the room, where he saw blinking red lights. Groton had set cameras that could see in the dark, that Rick instinctively knew were trained on Groton and Billy Dan. Starting with Billy Dan the same process that Groton had enticed Rick into.

Billy Dan spoke softly, haltingly through the grunts and groans of what Groton was doing to his cock.

"Somewhere where there are others, not in private. Somewhere public. And one man has followed me and has cornered me and is fondling me, making me want him."

"Yes, go on."

"But he is too big. Not long like you. Big like I'm afraid he'll split me. He scares as he crowds me. Doesn't let me think or give me time to consider. He is overpowering and I know he's going to get his way, and slowly but surely he does."

There was a pause there, as if that was all Billy Dan was going to say.

"There's more, isn't there? I can feel it in your cock. You can be harder, can reach the edge sooner. You just want to hold back. Tell me the rest. You said you were in public. Others were there. What were they doing while this man was seducing you?"

"They were looking, watching. Smiling and leering, leaning in to see everything. I know they would not have helped me if I didn't want what he was doing."

"But you did want it, didn't you? That's part of the release you need through this fantasy—admitting that what he was doing was exactly what you wanted him to do."

"Yeah, I guess so."

"And in the fantasy did these others just watch?"

A brief pause and then Billy Dan was whispering, "No."

"Ahh. Tell me, Billy. I can feel that you are on the edge. Say it. They didn't just watch. They took you too."

"Yes. Oh, shit. I'm gonna' blow. They took me too. One after the other. While the first man watched and laughed. But, damn, here I go."

"Yes, yes you are," Groton said. And then Rick felt him changing position on the bed—quickly. Moving down, and Billy Dan gave a heavy snort and let out a long, deep gasp as Groton covered his cock head with his mouth and took Billy Dan's essence. Groton came back up Billy Dan's body and they were kissing, sharing what had been coaxed out of the young man.

Then Billy Dan was on his belly and Groton was mounting his hips, and Rick too was riding the waves of the mattress, kept in motion by the rhythm of Groton riding Billy Dan's ass, while Billy Dan groaned and moaned.

Rick turned back toward the coupling pair on the bed. In the dimness of the light of the full moon coming through the slit in the red velour draperies, Rick could see Billy Dan's face. His eyes bore the expression of intense pleasure and his mouth was open, his tongue lolling out of it as he gave little sighing sounds.

He would be all right, Rick thought. He was enjoying it. This was something he'd chosen and was handling.

Billy Dan had come down in the middle of the bed and his face was mere inches from Rick's. The look he gave Rick was a signal that Rick instinctively responded to. Their lips met, and they kissed deeply as Groton rode on. And now Rick could taste the essence of Billy Dan as well.

Later in the night, Rick woke with a groan at the touch of Groton's hands on his hips, pulling his buttocks into Groton's midsection, his channel onto Groton's long, hard dick. Groton started slow fucking him.

"You did well today," he murmured in Rick's ear. "Tomorrow we leave for the Smokey Mountains."

"North Carolina?" Rick asked in a low voice.

"Or maybe Georgia or Texas. We need a very special bathtub."

Rick shuddered in anticipation, easily remembering the fantasy to be made reality.

Chapter Eight: Asheville

Rick was surprised to see Billy Dan standing by the Saab in the morning as they prepared to leave Lefty's. Rick had breakfasted with Phil and Roger and came out with them, moving toward the Dodge truck. But Groton called him over.

"You'll travel with us this, morning, Rick," he said and indicated one of the rear passenger doors. "You and Spike in back. I'll take Billy up front with me."

No other explanation than that as to why Billy Dan had joined the film group. And Lefty was just standing in the door of the roadhouse looking like he was just as pleased as punch to see his new boy waltzing off like that.

Then the possible explanation came to Rick, as Groton called back to Lefty while starting to drive out of the parking lot, "Have him back in a month or so—all trained and ready to go."

The two vehicles drove south in tandem on the road slicing down the small valley between the mountains and then turned up toward where the Wintergreen ski resort met the Blue Ridge Parkway running south and north across the crest of the mountains. Once up on the Parkway, Groton turned south. They hadn't gone far, though, when Groton turned into a picnic area visually separated from the parkway road. Groton's was the only car there; Phil drove the truck just off the road into the area and stopped, blocking the road enough that if another vehicle tried to come in, some time would be taken in accomplishing the maneuver. It was still early in the morning—too soon for anyone to want to be picnicking. The tops of the mountains were still covered with clouds, and there was an eerie quality to mist floating through the trees and across the lichen-encrusted rocks of the area.

"Let's see how well you can suck," Groton said in the front seat. Rick saw his hand go behind Billy Dan's head and draw it down toward his crotch. Shortly thereafter, Rick heard the arousing sounds of slurping and Groton's sighing as his head settled back on his headrest.

Spike, sitting close to Rick, his arm having been around his shoulder, drawing him to Spike on his side of the car and his hand busy in Rick's lap from the time the Saab started ascending the mountain at Wintergreen, signaled by the releasing of his hard cock and a hand on the back of Rick's head that Rick was to do the same on him as Billy Dan was doing on Groton. And Rick lowered his lips to Spike's thick, black cock and took him inside of his mouth, sucking at the bulb, as Spike sighed in satisfaction.

Rick lost track of what was going on in the front seat, and after Spike had stripped his trousers and briefs off him and while Spike was raising Rick up on his lap, facing the front, and slowly forcing Rick's channel down on his erection, Rick saw that they were finished in the front seat and now Groton was turned and capturing the backseat action with clicks of a still camera.

Rick didn't let that distract him. He was too busy trying to get all of Spike inside his channel and beginning to move his hips, playing off the balls of his feet on the floor of the car. Rick and Spike's last encounter alone had been interrupted, and out on the meadow the previous day, his was just one of several cocks inside Rick. The young man hadn't had the opportunity of the bittersweet fantasizing of Pete taking him for some time, which is what the ebony muscle-bound, big-cocked Spike did for him. Rick closed his eyes and conjured up Pete, hands on his waist and raising and lowering him on the cock that had given him so much frustration and pleasure in his early experience of taking.

When the filming team was ready to leave again, Groton had Spike sat up front, and Billy Dan was sent in the back with Rick.

They descended from the parkway into the Shenandoah valley at Buena Vista and caught I-81 south, headed for Ashville, North Carolina.

Once on the highway, Billy Dan shyly moved his hand to Rick's thigh and asked, in a whisper, whether he'd like to have a blow job too. But, with the best friendly and reassuring smile Rick could muster up, he said no thanks. Although Rick hadn't been able to see the resemblance between Billy Dan and him, others had and remarked on it. So, Rick considered Billy Dan as too much like him to be arousing in that way. Rick felt more protective of Billy Dan and didn't want to demean him to think Rick would make the demands on him or claims on his favors others did.

It was late afternoon before the two vehicles descended on I-26 through a mountain pass and the city of Asheville materialized below them in the bowl of surrounding mountains.

"Next stop," Groton sang out cheerily.

They drove through the town, which looked fresh and well-groomed and alive with people walking the sidewalks and continued, turning west from Montford on Hayward, toward the railroad tracks and a seedier part of town. Groton rolled up to a three-story row house, with a parking lot at one side where another, probably identical house, had given up the attempt to stand and had collapsed into its lot. On the other side of the building was a lower, two-story structure with a flashing neon sign over the door declaring "Baths."

Access to the door of the middle building, with the sign "Rooms" above it were stone steps bordered by concrete, broad-based parapets upon which sat an assortment of old and young men, lounging lazily, smoking, and watching those passing by.

The arrival of the two vehicles must have been the most exciting activity they'd seen that day, because their attention was uniformly riveted on the Saab and Dodge truck. The occupants disembarked and Spike and the cameramen started unloading luggage and camera equipment, as Groton mounted the stairs and entered the building. Billy Dan and Rick stood near the fender of the Saab, conversing with each other in close proximity and trying not to acknowledge the appraising looks they were getting from men sitting on the steps of the rooming house.

* * * *

It took some time for Rick to realize that the fantasy sequence was not to be his.

After settling into rooms at the boarding house, with Rick and Billy Dan again being shacked up with Groton in a room with a double and single bed and Rick disconcertedly being informed the twin bed was his, Groton met with the cameramen and then went around appraising and talking to other men in the rooming house. Then he was gone, on foot, for some time while Rick and the rest were left to fend for themselves.

Rick only left the room a couple of times, once to use the head down the hall and another time to go down to the first floor to check out on whether there were any vending machines or other possibility to get a Coke. On both outings, he was accosted at nearly every turn by one resident of the building after another, telling him how hot he looked and requesting or offering a blow job or, hopefully, more. Not wanting to offend or get into a bad situation, Rick told most of them some variation of "maybe later."

While downstairs he saw Billy Dan and another guy under the staircase in the shadows with Billy Dan on his knees and about to take the other guy's cock in his mouth when Spike showed up, manhandled Billy Dan off his knees, cuffed the other guy, and bustle Billy Dan up the stairs to the rooms there.

When Groton returned, the film team was being gathered up and walked next door to the two-story structure with the "Baths" sign.

As they entered, Rick assumed that Groton had found the bathtub he wanted to use for the filming of Rick's fantasy about that and was a little confused when Groton, already stripping told everyone else in the cast and crew, including Billy Dan, to strip, shower and go into the sauna. He told Phil and Roger they could put their briefs back on, as he was doing, but he told Spike, Billy Dan, and Rick to go into the sauna with towels around them.

There already were five other guys, just with towels, sitting in the sauna, so the six additions made for close quarters.

Groton pointed to the top level of the benches on the opposite wall from the entry door and Billy Dan went up there, apparently having received instructions beforehand, and stretched out on his back.

Groton pointed to the opposite corner of the sauna and told Rick to perch up there and watch.

That's when Rick realized that this was the filming of Billy Dan's fantasy spun out to Groton in bed the other night and not his fantasy of the bathtub. This was also the first time it dawned on Rick that he no longer was the sole star of this *Journey to Mirage* movie, but that now Billy Dan had been added to the cast. Rick wasn't sure what he thought about that, but as he sat there, watching Billy Dan's scene spin out, he also reflected on the bedding arrangements at Lefty's and now here, in Asheville, and he began to wonder—for the first time, but not the last time—if Groton was slowly supplanting him with Billy Dan. And he shuddered at the thought that his own scenes were becoming increasingly rough and threatening.

A guy in his mid forties was directed to sit on the top bench below Billy Dan's feet and the others—a guy in his twenties, two in their thirties, an older guy—all white—and then Spike were arranged around the sauna just outside the focus of Billy Dan stretched out and the older guy sitting below him. All of the men were in good shape and, although of distinctive looks, were quite presentable. The man sitting below Billy Dan was a hirsute guy with black hair—graying at the temples on his head but curly and pronounced on his chest, arms, and legs.

One of the thirtyish guys, blond marine cut, square-jawed, and gym sculpted, was sitting next to Rick.

Obviously rehearsed, Billy Dan began an act of enticement as the three cameramen took up positions at various angles. He had an arm thrown across his face as if he was in another world, but the man sitting below his feet slowly reached over and placed a hand on his ankle and Billy Dan did no more than slightly flinch. Thus encouraged, the man turned toward Billy Dan and took the other ankle in his other hand. Again, no countering reaction from Billy Dan.

The cameras panned to show that the other men in the room were taking notice now and turning their gazes to the action on the top bench on the back wall.

While his hands were still on Billy Dan's ankles, he spread the young man's legs to the limit of the wide depth of bench and made an obvious, satisfied inspection of what he could see up under Billy Dan's towel. Slowly, the man's hands glided up Billy Dan's calves, over his knees, and a short distance up his thighs, almost, but not quite, reaching the hemline of the towel around Billy Dan's waist.

Billy Dan moaned loud enough for the cameras to pick up. And the other men in the sauna began to pair off—only in moving closer to someone else at this point.

Rick wasn't left out of this. The blond marine type was close enough to him now that their thighs touched. His towel fell open and Rick looked down to find a nice-sized half hard cock nestling between the man's meaty thighs.

The cameras were panning the sauna but came back to focus on Billy Dan and the man sitting below him, who was moving his hands back to Billy Dan's ankles and, when there, gently, ever so slowly and gently folding Billy Dan's up so that they were spread, bent, and Billy Dan was digging the heels of his feet into the wet teak of the bench.

The man put his hands on Billy' Dan's knees and spread his legs wider. His attention was riveted on what he now could see under the spread towel between Billy Dan's thighs. Groton moved his camera to where he was looking over the man's shoulder and enjoying the same view he had.

Once again the man's hands started a slow guide up Billy Dan's inner thighs, as Billy Dan groaned.

Rick looked away then, though, because he had to look down at his own lap, where the blond marine type had opened his towel and encased his cock with a slow-pumping hand. The blond lowered his face to Rick's and they kissed, after which, the blond moved his mouth down the hollow of Rick's neck and to his nipples.

The man across the sauna had moved in closer to Billy Dan's bent knees and his hands were up under the towel. The towel was moving at Billy Dan's crotch, leaving no doubt what the man's hands were doing under there. Billy Dan groaned and lifted the leg that was closest to the wall and hooked it over the man's shoulder.

There were moans and groans elsewhere in the sauna too, as the two other couples that had paired up became more intimate, while all the time paying close attention to what was happening with Billy Dan. The older guy and the other thirtyish guy were sitting side by side, each with the other's cock in a fist. Spike had already moved way ahead of everyone else. He had the twentyish guy in his lap, facing away from him, already working his channel with his cock, while Spike fisted and slow pumped the young guy's cock.

The cameras were everywhere, taking it all in.

Billy Dan's partner now had his head under the towel, Billy Dan holding it with both of his hands through the material of the towel, and arching his back and making guttural noises. His face, wearing an expression of ecstasy, was turned toward the center of the sauna. Phil's camera was focused on the expression. His knot of his towel at last parted and the towel fell away to reveal the man deep-throating his cock. Billy Dan lurched and shuddered and gave a little cry and the man came off his cock and turned Billy Dan on his stomach and began to separate his butt cheeks with hands and to go after Billy Dan's hole with his mouth.

Another cry was heard in the sauna as the twenty-something guy came. Spike continued raising and lowering the guy's channel on his cock, though.

A third cry out represented the blond marine type lifting Rick and setting Rick's channel down on his cock, Rick facing him and his legs splayed out outside the man's arms, his feet pushing at the cedar wood paneling of the sauna wall. The marine type had Rick's waist encased in his strong hands and was pulling Rick up and down on his cock.

The other couple parted, with the older guy hopping up on the bench at Billy Dan's head and lapping Billy Dan's face, with Billy Dan's mouth sliding over his cock. The other man was straddling Billy Dan's hips now and deep stroking his ass from above and behind.

The other thirtyish guy went to Rick and the Marine type. Taking Rick by the shoulders, he bent the young man back so that his back ran down the Marine type's legs. The thirtyish guy slipped his cock between Rick's lips as, bent all the way back toward the floor, Rick grabbed the back of the guy's calves and took cock at both ends.

Spike was up now, pushing Billy Dan's first partner aside and replacing him in fucking Billy Dan.

Groton slipped off his briefs and put his camera down and turned the twenty-something Spike had been fucking to where he was bent over the bench, facing the wall, and Groton mounted him and began to stroke.

And now the orgy on Billy Dan's body started in full.

Finished with Rick, who sat back as far as he could in the corner and watched, the two men who had been cocking him, left him and went and stood in line behind the older man, who had been worked up to want more of Billy Dan than his mouth and had come down and sat on the lower bench beside Spike's legs, waiting for his turn with Billy Dan's ass.

Spike had Billy Dan up on his hands and knees and was fucking him doggy style. And then, one after the other, the other men in line—the original man for a second time—took Billy Dan in a fulfillment of the fantasy he had spun for Groton.

Groton had finished with the twenty-something guy, who just sat on the bench in a panting heap and when the cameraman Roger indicated an interest, signaled his acquiescence. Roger put down his camera and Groton took it up. And Roger's cock was the last one inside Billy Dan.

It was not lost on Rick that Phil had not requested or claimed a taking.

* * * *

"Have you no fantasy for me?" Groton was whispering in Rick's ear later that night. He had come into the room late, after Billy Dan and Rick had gone to bed and, to Rick's surprise, had come over to the twin bed rather than to the double. Two video cameras were set up on stands, but they hadn't been pointed at either of the beds until Groton came in and set them focused on the twin bed.

Rick realized that he needed to come up with something, but he was exhausted and confused—and not knowing how he felt about Billy Dan increasingly being brought into play.

"I'm tired, Mr. Groton. Oh so tired. Give me a minute or two." Rick moved his hand down to where Groton was working his cock and put his hand over Groton's. Something inside him told him it was important to keep Groton there. To spin a fantasy for him. But reality had been so overwhelming that it was becoming increasingly difficult to have unfulfilled dreams.

"They used to be right on your tongue, Rick. I'm not sure a forced or a false fantasy with do."

"Just . . ." Rick's mind raced over encounters with Pete and Tony. Something fresh, he needed a fresh and different concept.

"Pity," Groton whispered, as he stopped stroking and rose on the bed.

"No, don't go," Rick whimpered, trying to hold onto Groton as the man slipped away from him.

Rick listened in terror and consternation as it began in the other bed.

"Indians," Billy Dan murmured. "It's the old West and I've been taken by a band of Indians. Nearly naked savages. In war paint and all. Loincloths, moccasins, and war paint."

"And how do they treat you? Are they belligerent, threatening?"

"No, not really. Not in the dream. They are almost jovial. Touching me, passing me back and forth between them."

"And they fuck you?"

"No, not them. As they are teasing me, another brave rides up. Magnificent in the saddle. Obviously a leader among them."

"And?"

"And he says something to them and they all laugh. And he rolls his hips back so that his buttock is resting on the buttocks of the horse and I see that he is naked—and had a big hard on, curving to the sky."

"And he comes down off the horse . . .?"

"No, this is the thing of the fantasy. The other braves lift me up in front of him on the horse, bent over so my arms and legs hang down on the sides."

"And he thrusts inside you?"

"Yes, yes he does. And then he spurs the horse into a half gallop and we're racing across the plains and the gait of the horse is moving . . . Oh, shit. I'm there. I'm gonna cum."

"Yes, yes you are."

"And the gait of the horse moves his cock inside me and my ass slides back and forth on the cock and . . . Oh, geezz, here it comes."

All was soon quiet in the room, except for the sounds of Groton side-splitting Billy Dan and Billy Dan loving every stroke of it.

Rick lay there, awake, knowing somehow that tonight Groton would not be visiting him again after he was finished with Billy Dan. Knowing that Billy Dan, through no knowledge or fault of his own, had moved one step closer to supplanting Rick. And, worse, realizing that Phil had been right—that Rick had formed no "after this" plan.

Chapter Nine: New Orleans

The scene filmed in the bathhouse sauna had left a fearful impression on Rick. Even though it hadn't been the reality scene he thought had been meant for him, after his initial shock of so much intense coupling developing before him, Rick had been caught up in the orgy nature of it almost as much as Billy Dan had been. Rick had become lost in the throes of the event, having been taken himself and then watching Billy Dan being cocked numerous times. In some ways, the scene in the sauna was more of a never-ending violation of innocence, with Rick doing nothing but joining in, than the scene in the meadow had been. This was largely because as each man took up a position crouching over Billy Dan's body, Rick had thought about it being him—had almost salivated for it to be him—until the older man had seen the effect it was having on Rick and mounted the bench in front of him, roughly slapped his thighs apart, grabbed and spread-eagled his ankles, and then was giving Rick what Rick couldn't help but wanting.

Phil had briefly come over, prepared to pull the old man off Rick if Rick signaled that's not what he wanted. But Rick didn't signal that.

After it was all over, though, Rick had sought Phil out and apologized.

"Apologies for what?" Phil said.

"For giving in like that in the Sauna. For not being able to control myself."

97

"As you've said, it's your life and your decision," Phil said.

Despite this license by Phil, however, in which Rick hadn't detected any enthusiasm, in those last few days before everything fell apart, Rick did try for some form of restraint. And to help himself strive for that, he stayed as close as he could to Phil. He figured as long as he was near Phil, he would be doing what was expected for him and no more.

Groton helped him in this respect. That night, Groton never left the bed Billy Dan was occupying to come to Rick's bed.

"Close your eyes and imagine," Groton was whispering to Billy Dan from the other bed as their bodies were entwined and Groton was slowly masturbating Billy Dan. Two video cameras facing the bed on stands are whirring softly. "Where are you in your fantasy?"

"I'm on the roof of a building in a city," Billy Dan murmured.

"Alone?"

"No, I have been told there is something he wants me to see on the roof of the building. He is the superintendent of the building, and I lived there—with my boyfriend. But my boyfriend isn't there, and this man is at my door, saying he has something to show me on the roof."

"And was it his cock that he has to show you when you get to the roof?"

"Yeah."

"And he fucks you on the roof?"

"Yeah."

"Just the two of you?"

"The building is lower than the ones around it. It's in the middle of the day. A working day."

"And what you are doing draws an audience to you from the windows of the surrounding buildings?"

"Yeah."

"Do you enjoy the fucking?"

"No. He is rough. And he smells of garlic. I have not wanted it and he's had to trap me and wrestle me to the tarpapered floor of the roof."

"Is he violent?"

"He hits me a couple of times. I'm dazed and this makes me stop struggling as he pins me to the top of a skylight with his cock inside me. I look down through the skylight and men in the room below are looking up, watching him fuck me."

"Does no one help you?"

"A policeman comes . . . but . . . but . . ."

"But he fucks you too after the other man has finished?"

"Yeah, he does."

"And you want him?"

"Yeah, yeah, I do. It's special with the uniform—him bein' a cop."

"Is that all?"

A pause as Billy Dan moaned deeply, Rick not knowing whether it's because he was close to coming under the attention of Groton's hand or whether it was from some fantasized element of his story.

"He has a billy club . . ."

"And he uses it on you?"

"Yeah."

"And then there are the men from the room below the skylight?"

"Yeah."

For a reason Rick could not identify, he didn't want to hear Billy Dan's ejaculation, so he covered his head with his pillow—and waited for Groton to finish fucking Billy Dan and then to come for him.

But Groton didn't come into his bed, and Rick went to sleep thinking if he could just stay close to Phil tomorrow—Groton having said they'd be here one more day—maybe he could start bringing some level of calm, dignity—and backbone—back into his life.

And maybe tomorrow was the day he could confront Groton over some sort of regular pay. Groton was covering Rick's room and board and giving him a few bills here and there when Rick asked for them—and he had replaced any clothes that had been ripped off Rick's body during scene filming. But thus far Rick hadn't received the thousands of dollars Groton had told him he'd be paid. He still had the nest egg he'd come with, but Phil had remonstrated with him more than once that he needed to be paid more regularly and substantially by Groton as they journeyed toward the film festival in Mirage, that he couldn't trust Groton to pay him in full what he'd agreed to pay only when they'd reached Arizona.

Maybe, Rick thought, Phil would be there when Rick broached the subject with Groton. Maybe Phil would give Rick the confidence to make his claim.

* * * *

When Rick woke, he thought he was alone in the room. It was late morning, and whenever he had slept in before, Groton and Billy Dan had already gone down to breakfast.

The room was still fairly dark, because the curtains on the window were heavy, but they didn't meet squarely in the middle, so there was a strong beam of light, heavy with dust particles, streaming across the room and onto the other bed.

Rick heard the sounds of the groaning and slurping and he followed the cast of the sunbeam to find Billy Dan still curled up on the bed, but his hands raised, holding Spike's naked buttocks close to him, as he serviced Spike's cock. Spike's hands were on the back of Billy Dan's head, guiding the young blond's motion, and Spike was holding what Rick could tell were leather restraints in his hands as well.

"Spike," Rick called out in surprise. "Where's Mr. Groton? You know he won't want—"

"Doug and the cameramen have gone into downtown Asheville to look for film supplies. He told me to look after you two until he got back."

Phil. Phil wasn't here, Rick thought, in panic. But what he said was, "I don't think this is what he meant by looking after us."

"You can stay here and watch or not," Spike said gruffly. "Billy here wants me to fuck him. Don't you Billy?"

There was a murmur of "yeah" from the bed.

"You want me to bind you to the bed and punish your ass, don't you?"

A whimpered "yeah."

Rick curled up in the corner of his bed and watched in mixed concern and envy as Rick tied Billy Dan's wrists together over his head and at the slats of the headboard; scooted his knees under Billy Dan's buttocks, raising the young man's pelvis to him; and, holding Billy Dan's legs out wide, spiked his ass with that thick, long, black cock of his and pumped in slow, deep strokes, as Billy Dan writhed under him and breathily repeated over and over again how much he was enjoying the cocking by the big, black stud.

When Rick couldn't take anymore of watching Billy Dan getting what he ached for, he tumbled off the bed and raced down the hall to the bath at the end of the hall. He turned on the shower and stood under the stream of water, trying to drown out the memory of the sounds of Billy Dan begging for more of Spike's cocking.

"You really want to shower alone, pretty boy?"

Rick turned and saw that the shower door was fully blocked out by a leering Hispanic of gigantic proportions.

The young man went down on his knees on the wet tile floor in front the Hispanic monster and took the bulb of his cock his mouth and cupped the man's heavy-hanging balls in his hand.

The Hispanic fucked Rick against the tile wall of the shower, the water streaming over their steaming bodies, with Rick's legs hooked on the man's hips and the power of the man's cock pushing Rick's back up and down on the slick, soap-encrusted tiles of the shower wall. Another Hispanic man entered the bath and Rick opened his legs for him as well.

All of the time, Rick's mind was flipping back and forth between wishing it was him bound on the bed with Spike's cock working inside him and cursing Phil for not being there and helping him to stifle those thoughts, desires, and instincts.

* * * *

When Rick returned to the rooming house room, Spike was still fucking Billy Dan—or was doing it again, or for the third time. And he was splitting him so totally that Billy Dan's eyes were cloudy with cum and he was almost unconscious with exhaustion and was moaning lowly.

Spike left before Groton returned, but when Groton did return and entered the room, Billy Dan was still lying on the back, legs spread, and moaning. It was obvious to Groton that someone had been at the young man. He looked at Rick, huddled back on his own bed, reading magazines, and Rick just shrugged and said, "It wasn't me. I'm sure you can figure it out."

Groton left the room again and Rick waited for a half hour before dressing in jeans and a T and venturing forth. Only Roger was downstairs, in the dining room, when Rick entered.

"Where's everyone?" Rick asked.

"Phil's up in his room, I think," Roger answered. "Doug and Spike have gone back out. Doug said he had more to do in town."

Rick stood around for a few minutes, shuffling his feet and deciding whether he wanted to eat or go back to his room, but it didn't take long for him to decide to go back upstairs. The two Hispanics from the shower were there in the dining room, sitting at a table with three other guys. They all were taking furtive glances at Rick and exchanging words punctuated with low-toned laughs. Rick felt like he was being undressed with their eyes, and, Groton having made him fantasy prone, he was beginning to have a vision of them coming for him and slamming him down on a table top and taking turns with him. Somehow he didn't think that Roger would do anything to prevent that. Most likely, judging by his performance in the sauna the previous day, he would be the second one slamming his cock up into Rick's channel and then would stand back and film the rest of it.

Rick turned and went up the stairs again. But he didn't go to Groton's room. He walked right on beyond that and stood in front of Phil's door for almost a minute before knocking on it.

"Come in," Phil's voice rang out from the other side.

Rick was filled with relief. Phil was here. He'd be safe now.

He entered the room. Phil, just in shorts, was sitting at a small desk and writing a letter or a note.

"Rick," he said, as the young man entered the room.

"I couldn't think of anywhere else to go," Rick said. "I wanted to be safe. So I came here."

Phil rose. He had a pained expression on his face.

"You won't be safe here, I'm afraid, Rick. I can't take it anymore. I won't be able to keep my hands off you unless you leave now. Right now."

"Then don't even try," Rick whispered, his heart leaping in his chest. "I want to stay."

They came together like two freight trains mistakenly shunted off onto the same track. As they hungrily kissed, Phil's fingers went to Rick's T and then to his jeans zipper as Rick's hands went to the snaps on Phil's shorts.

Phil encased both of their cocks together, and the two stood there, trying to meld into the other, still in a deep kiss, as Rick's hands palmed Phil's buttocks and his fingernails dug into yielding flesh there.

Phil pushed Rick down onto his back on the bed and then he knelt between Rick's thighs and made love to Rick's cock and balls with his mouth until, with a cry, Rick exploded in a gush of cum. Then, turning Rick on his side and lifting his leg to his shoulder, Phil fucked Rick's hole in a side split while they conveyed the totality of the fuck with their eyes locked on each other.

"I'm sorry, I couldn't leave without this," Phil murmured, as they lay on the bed, their bodies stretched along each other's as closely entwined as they could manage, Rick's buttocks cuddled into Phil's crotch.

"Leave?" Rick moaned. "You can't."

"I have to. I can't watch this happening to you anymore. I wouldn't be here with you, like this, now, if I wasn't going to leave. I can't be any part of this. I'll leave you my cell phone number. Anytime you want to pull away from this, call. And I'll come get you."

"I can—"

"No, I don't think you can . . . yet. But I hope that someday you will."

"Please, don't leave. I'll—"

"I promise I won't leave in the next twenty minutes. In fact, my cock's going to be so far up in your channel and making such complete love to you that you'll forget all about my leaving."

"Oh, god. Yesssss! Oh, shitttt! Mooaaan. I've . . . it's never been like this . . . before." Rick turned his face to Phil, and they went into a deep kiss, every other point in their bodies trying to merge, become one . . . forever, but Phil resolved that it would only be for the next twenty minutes.

* * * *

The next morning was like a whirlwind. Groton hadn't come back to the room that night, but when Rick went downstairs the next morning—walking on air, because the hour he'd spent with Phil the previous day was the closest he'd ever come to a love-based merging—Groton was there, in the dining room, looking both disheveled and livid.

He was holding a letter—which Rick recognized as what Phil had been writing when Rick went to his room. Groton waved it in Roger's face and was babbling almost incoherently. Or at least it seemed incoherent to Rick at first, because, as he saw the letter, he remembered what Phil had said about leaving, the blood rushed to his ears, and he had to sit down in the nearest chair to keep from fainting.

"The worst possible time," Groton was growling. "And he really gives no reason. Now we'll be delayed. I need another cameraman and I need to think whether Spike needs to be replaced or not."

He calmed down a bit then, though. "Perhaps it's all for the best. I need to review what we have already, to do a first cut on that—and it's time to pick up someone to help me with that, someone who can hold a camera as well and keep his pants zipped. Here's as good a place as any, I guess, to do a first cut of what we have. Go up and roust out Billy Dan, though, and get these two packing up. One thing I know is that there's too much going on here and now I'll have to move them and find someone to watch over them—no, don't even suggest it, Roger—I've seen what little restraint you have."

"Replace Spike?" Rick asked in a faraway voice, having caught at least that much of Groton's rant. "What is this about replacing Spike?"

"I put him on a train back to Baltimore last night. I don't want to lose his talents forever, but he was paid to perform for the camera, not to mess up the goods off camera. Now go on upstairs and get your things together. You're moving someplace else. There're too many randy guys around here, and I know you've been putting out for them for free too."

Somewhere else turned out to be a rundown motel several miles out of Asheville to the west. While Roger was checking Rick and Billy Dan in, Groton went off and returned with a fat middle-aged black guy who looked like bad business. He looked every inch a seedy club bouncer, which, undoubtedly was what he was at night.

Billy Dan and Rick were locked in the motel room and the fat black guy sat down on a chair in front of the door and under the overhang between the motel building and the parking lot.

Rick settled down, turning on the TV and flipping channels until something half interesting showed up, but Billy Dan started fidgeting and pacing back and forth almost immediately. He obviously didn't like being cooped up and just as obviously was in need for something else.

Rick watched Billy Dan pace and mutter under his breath with both concern and disgust. Was this what he too had been reduced to—being used so often in so many different ways in fantasies he himself had voiced that it had become an addiction, that he couldn't get enough of it often enough?

Surely not. Rick reasoned that he didn't need it now, wasn't in some sort of sweating frustration like Billy Dan was for the lack of it. But then, he'd been with Phil just the previous day. And it had been very different with Phil. Rick felt completely satisfied with Phil's fucking—like he didn't need anything but that, and from Phil only. He thought that there could be so much more to it with Phil than just the physical scratching of an itch, a temporary fix of a need.

Billy Dan was at Rick to do something with him, but Rick still felt like doing it with Billy Dan—even letting the guy suck him off—would be like a masturbation of himself that brought no satisfaction. They were too much alike. Maybe if Rick wasn't still in an afterglow of his afternoon with Phil . . .

The times the fat black guy came in to use the can were also opportunities for Billy Dan to offer himself, to beg. But the guy wasn't having any of that. He probably didn't even like men, which was evident from the disdainful look he gave Billy Dan.

At last Billy Dan's itch was scratched, though, when Groton came to the motel, all smiles and walking on air because of what he considered a success both in someone who could help him edit the films and would stand in as a cameraman but also because of how well the film he had reviewed and begun to edit was falling into place.

"Got a winner here," he said to Rick, as Billy Dan sank to his knees in front of Groton and began scrabbling as the man's trouser zipper.

Groton took him missionary style on one of the double beds, Billy Dan clutching Groton's waist tightly with his legs and giving little yipping sounds at the depth at which Groton was stroking him, while Rick watched a European soccer game on the TV. He knew nothing about the teams and little about the sport, but he gave the TV set all of the attention he could to try to wipe out the sounds from the other bed.

Rick was fidgeting now himself and felt like pacing the room, but he forced himself to concentrate on the TV and didn't even identify the source of his frustration until after Groton was finished with Billy Dan, who laid there on one of two double beds in the motel room, bedspread and sheets tussled, legs akimbo, moaning in satisfaction and at least temporary satiation of need. Groton left without even touching Rick, and the disappointment Rick felt as Groton closed the door behind him caused him to tremble with fear at the realization that deep down—and maybe not so deep down—he was no different at all from Billy Dan. Only the thought of Phil had stood in the way of that. But Phil was gone now, and the memory of their afternoon was beginning to recede.

If only Phil had stayed—or, better yet, had taken Rick with him.

Late in the night, when Rick, still awake and fretting, heard the door to the motel room quietly open and felt the bulk of the fat black man, somehow having become naked between the door and the bed, come down heavily on top of him; the man's hand going over his mouth to keep him silent, his hot, sour breath and his musky in-heat man scent mingling to both repel and entice Rick's senses, Rick felt no compulsion to scream or reject whatsoever. To the man's surprise and heightening lust, Rick reached down and took the man's thick, hard cock and balls in his hands, knowing it would be black and as strong as Spike's—and Pete's—spread his legs and hooked his heels over the base of the man's bulging buttocks, rolled his hips up, and guided the hot cock into his channel. As his channel awakened and undulated over the cock as it drew the member slowly in and the man groaned and grunted and panted his unexpected good fortune, his hand still over Rick's mouth, but a thumb having been sucked in between Rick's lips, images of Spike and then of Pete raced through Rick's mind. Rick tried to think of Phil as well, but what was happening now was no part of Phil's world.

This was the devil of need inside him he had fought so hard to convince himself had no control over him.

Chapter Ten: Dallas

Rick, stretched out on the double bed nearest the door, heard voices outside—it was the familiar sound of Groton's voice that had awakened him—far earlier than anyone should be stirring. Rick looked over at the clock on the bedside table, saw that it was still 5:30 AM, and he groaned and turned on his back, legs spread. His channel was sore. The bodyguard had been thorough and long lasting. The thought that had come into his mind was that Billy Dan would have liked that. But he snored through the whole taking, and the man had been fully satisfied with what he'd gotten from Rick and had returned to his vigil outside the door, after visiting the can, without molesting Billy Dan as well.

Rick came fully awake when he heard Groton laugh and ask, "Good ass, wasn't he? Sweet enough for you?"

Rick didn't hear the reply but he was already building an irk. He had wondered if Groton would find out that the dog put on guard duty last night had been in the hen house himself. Now he knew. This probably had been the agreed-upon payment for the bodyguard's services. He certainly knew that Groton did use money as payment any time he could get away with not doing so. And Rick wondered if part of the agreement was that the bodyguard would leave Billy Dan alone. Certainly Groton was showing far more jealousy now about what was done with Billy Dan away from the cameras than he was about Rick.

Not much question that Rick was earning his way on the trip in more ways than one, and he knew that this wouldn't be the last travel expense he was supposed to carry. What Phil had said about Groton going ahead and selling still shots on the Internet as they traveled across the country had sunk in. Groton traveled with a laptop and when Rick saw him downloading photos onto a Web site one afternoon, he called him out on what he was doing.

"Publicity," Groton had said. "Most of these are stills from the movie shots. I want the men clamoring to see *Journey to Mirage* even before we reach the festival. It will help in the voting."

But, as Phil had said, Rick knew that it was helping in getting them across country to Mirage as well. That part of this operation was no mirage to Rick. Phil had opened his eyes to that—and then he had opened Rick to so much more. But then that door had been slammed shut.

Groton bounced into the room, turning on lights and literally pulling a groggy Billy Dan out of the bed.

"Up and dressed, boys. I'm taking you to Mardi Gras in New Orleans, and it's a good chug away from here. We need to be on the road."

Rick and Billy Dan stumbled out of the room into the chill mountain air just before six, both complaining about needing breakfast, both being ignored.

"We'll stop on the road—drive you through a drive through," Groton announced cheerily. "Both of you in the Saab."

It would be just three of them in the Saab now, Groton's film crew having been decimated. But Rick looked over and saw that there was someone else standing by the Dodge truck now, someone to ride with Roger. No introductions were made until they stopped for lunch, but then Rick learned his name was Howard. He was an obvious computer geek—sallow skin and thin, undeveloped body, presumably from sitting in front of a computer his every waking moment, and bottle-thick eye glasses, no doubt brought about by the same consuming interest in computer programming. Other than that, he didn't look too bad. But it looked like even Billy Dan could easily break him in two with his hands, and even Billy Dan showed him no interest, treating him like he wasn't in the troupe at all. So, Rick thought, maybe Groton had signed on the ideal film assistant for his needs and who would assuage his worries at last.

* * * *

It was nearly 7:00 PM before they managed to get to the small hotel Groton had somehow been able to finagle rooms in during Mardi Gras in New Orleans. The last hour of travel was spent in trying to drive through the crowds of costumed revelers in the streets of the old city. The hotel was in the French Quarter, at its northern edge, but just barely.

The hotel wasn't right on the street, but down an alley barely wide enough to accommodate the Dodge truck. Then, at the hotel's entry passageway, the vehicles had to negotiate a sharp right turn through another passageway into a small parking lot, where at one time there must have been a building.

It was growing dark and torches were already lit. Revelers were out on Barracks Street en masse, most of them headed for the more-central Bourbon Street area. As Rick and the others approached the entry door, trudging because they were so tired from the long drive and the frustration of the last hour just trying to get into the city, eerie silhouettes of garishly costumed celebrants were cast over the ochre-colored cut stone of the hotel front. A bunch of clowns—obviously all part of the same group—were milling around in the forecourt of the hotel. They thumped on the trunks and hoods of the cars hovering somewhere between the comical, the grotesque, and the marginally scary, while Groton's band disembarked.

The first order of business once Groton's men had entered the hotel was something to eat, and they found the hotel's dining room filled with half-costumed patrons, hurriedly wolfing down their food so that they themselves could pour out into the streets for a party that would go until dawn. Just dropping into the scene like this provided a specter for Groton's little band of a wild masque of excess from an earlier century.

Groton turned quite jovial and he ordered extra wine for the table.

"Eat and drink up, lads, and then a snooze. A short one, though, as we have work to do."

The owner of the hotel appeared at Groton's side at the end of the meal. He was a double-chinned man of large size and dressed expansively and flamboyantly in a black silk suit with a frilled white shirt and sporting a handle-bar mustache that had been waxed and curled at the end a la Salvador Dali. The man himself was so theatrical that Rick rather thought the attire was his everyday choice and not donned especially for Mardi Gras. All smiles and puffed up, he greeted Groton as an old friend, and, scanning the table, asked with a broad smile, "Who is it to be?"

That's when Rick found out how they had managed to get the rooms for Mardi Gras on such short notice.

Groton pointed to Rick, and the hotel owner nearly salivated in his show of appreciation. He had two room keys in his hand, which he gave to Groton. Groton, in turn, gave one to Roger. And that was how it was to be. Groton and Billy Dan were sleeping in one room and Roger and the new film assistant, Howard, were in the other. Rick was in the hotel owner's room, and Groton was motioning him to rise and go with the man now.

"I will require him for a couple of hours after midnight, Alphonse. But until then he's yours. Use him as you will."

Being "used" by the rotund Spaniard turned out not to be as taxing as Rick had been afraid it would be. The Spaniard wanted him to strip and stand before him for several moments, as he savored the moment. Then he walked around and around Rick, touching him and playing his tongue over Rick's body.

After that he wanted to play with and suck Rick's cock and balls more intimately and had Rick lay on his back on the bed, while slowly, ever so slowly—slowed even more by Rick's exhaustion from the road trip—the hotelier used his fingers and tongue and teeth to bring Rick to the edge of ejaculation and then away from the edge again and back—until Rick could hold it no more and flowed in a long sigh.

The Spaniard wanted to fuck then. But he wanted Rick to do all of the work. He lay on the bed on his back and Rick had to mount and ride his cock.

Mercifully, it was just the once, though, and it was all over quickly. By the time the Spaniard had come, he appeared to be as tired a Rick was, and he drifted quickly off into a loud-snoring sleep. Rick rolled off him and to the side, and he was fast asleep as well.

* * * *

Shortly after midnight, Groton entered the room and roused Rick and pulled him away. He was dressed as a seventeenth-century buccaneer and he had a costume for Rick too—tight silk pants, with black boots, and a pull-over blousy white cotton shirt that opened almost to his navel, the wide opening showing much of his chest and being laced together with white string.

Billy Dan wasn't dressed. He was lolling in Groton's bed, legs spread wide, his eyes with the dazed look he had after he'd been worked over by Groton's ten-inch cock, which, no doubt he just had been.

Roger and Howard were standing out in the hall, dressed all in black, with black face masks, and hoisting video cameras. Roger had two, one in each hand.

"What's Billy Dan—?" Rick started to say.

"He's not going with us tonight," Groton said. "This is your filming."

Rick tried to remember what scene this might be—and when he did, the image of the group of intimidating clowns that had accosted them in the hotel's forecourt, he shuddered and considered trying to beg off.

"Come. I've found just the club we need," Groton said and, before Rick could try to think of a reason they couldn't be doing this, they were walking through the entranceway and into the tunneled drive and out to the noise and hullabaloo on Barracks Street.

Groton didn't lead the group farther into the French Quarter, though. He led them northeast, along Dauphine Street, toward the docks area. Entering Burgundy Street, which was almost deserted, the main activity of the evening being in the nearby French Quarter, the raucous noise of which followed them into the dark streets around the docks, Groton stopped at a set of iron steps rising up to an old brick building, which looked to be totally deserted. There was a yellow light showing through the lacy iron stair treads up to the main entrance door, though, and Groton dipped around the stairs to the left to other stairs that led down into a well under the landing. He knocked on the wooden door that was one story directly under the main entrance, which opened, revealing an eerie, smoky half-lit room beyond.

It was some sort of bar. All of the patrons were in costumes—all sorts of ghoulish dress, predominated by black capes and sinister vampire-looking characters. All of them appeared to be men, and all of them locked their eyes on Rick as the group entered. Roger and Howard instinctively shrank into the shadows around the wall, where their black dressing made them virtually invisible. Groton held Rick at arm's length as he moved into the room, showing the young man off. In homage to this offering, a cleared circle opened around the two as they walked and all eyes followed their progress.

A table in the middle of the room cleared for them, the patrons obviously all preferring the shadows around the periphery themselves. Groton parked Rick here and went to the bar, where he spoke briefly with a heavyset man sitting at the far end. Money was exchanged and Groton came back and sat down beside Rick.

All eyes were still on them, while the heavyset man drew several men around him, who then fanned out in the crowd.

A series of men in black capes—all striving for the vampire effect—were brought to the table for Groton's inspection. At length, he picked three, all tall and well-built and of sinister dark-featured countenances. He spoke briefly with them, holding his wallet in his hand until he was satisfied he had the best deal closed—and after he'd made them all bare their chests and lower their trousers. He picked the one with the best mix of build and cock size.

"Where?" Rick heard him say.

With a broad smile, the man answered as he readjusted his clothing, "St. Louis Number Two should do fine. It's farther away than Number One, but not as close to the Quarter. It should be deserted tonight. And we can reach it on foot."

When he smiled, Rick shuddered. His canine teeth where protruding and sharpened. There was no clue whether they were fakes or implants.

It proved to be a rather long walk, southwest on Rampart to St. Louis and then northwest four blocks to the edge of the route 10 superhighway.

Groton instructed the vampire—for that was what the man fancied himself to be whether he was or not—and Howard to stop just inside the gates to the cemetery while he and Roger led Rick down the concrete paths between the raised tombs until he'd found the tomb he wanted. He told Rick to climb up on the tomb. Rick started to say something to Groton, but Groton spat back, "It's your fantasy. And we can't be long. Someone could come back at almost any time. Now, hop up on the top of the tomb and take a willing sacrifice's pose."

Groton had chosen the raised tomb he did because there were iron rings embedded in the concrete at each edge of the tabletop tomb. Rick laid back on the cold, hard surface on his back, as Groton on one side and Roger at the other took two-foot-long chains out of a bag Roger had carried into the cemetery and attached them to Rick's wrists and then to each ring on the sides, pulling his arms above his head. The chains they used on his ankles and the rings at the bottom of the tomb tope were four feet long, giving length for Rick's legs to be raised and spread—but not for him to be able to escape his bonds.

Groton and Roger, video cameras in hand backed off from each side of the tomb, and Rick heard Groton's soft whistle.

The whistle was the cue for the vampire, who slowly and deliberately—a bit too theatrically, Rick thought—began to stride into the cemetery and toward the tomb atop which Rick was now spread-eagled and chained. Other than the black cape billowing around his body and his black boots, the vampire now was completely nude.

Groton had picked well. His body was well worked and muscle hard. There was little fat on him, but he wasn't lean either. He was of dusky complexion, and the distinctive blackness and prodigious size of his cock and balls, swinging low and free between his thighs as he walked attested to mixed heritage.

As the cameras whirred, he strode purposely to the base of the tomb and lithely bounded on top of it. It almost appeared that he had floated up to where he was standing over Rick, who was writhing within the limits of his chains on the tomb top and looking appropriately frightened. Howard appeared in the shadows below the tomb, giving a third-angle shot.

Groton, muttering his delight at the mystery and dexterity by which the vampire mounted the tomb—which only would need a bit of change in film speed at that point to give the illusion of floating—and blessing the mood being enhanced by the heavy mist beginning to filter into the cemetery, moved around to the head of the tomb to get the full frontal shot of the naked, barring the billowing black cape, vampire, showing his toothy smile and looking down at his tomb-top captive, his wickedly upcurved erection showing his approval of the night's sacrificial lamb.

Then exhibiting his long, sharp fingernails, the would-be vampire proceeded to slice Rick's clothing off his body, all the time rubbing the underside of his curved cock on Rick's belly.

Rick turned his head from the sight of his clothing being slowly slashed away and arched his back, fighting ineffectively against his bonds, perhaps partially as an act, but almost wholly at the horror of what the fantasy of several nights previously had produced.

Dramatically, the vampire came down on his knees on either side of Rick's chest and, grabbing Rick's head roughly in his hands, assaulted his mouth with a hard cock. Rick gagged and groaned and thrashed about as the vampire thrust into his throat, pulling Rick's head back and forth on the cock.

At length, fully engorged, the vampire moved his knees back down to between Rick's spread knees, and he had the palms of his hands under Rick's buttocks, pulling the cheeks apart and squeezing the orbs. A camera panned in as a forefinger of each hand invaded Rick's channel as Rick, panting, breathing hard, and crying out at the invasion of his channel by sharp fingernails, arched his back and moaned hard.

The vampire displayed his cock entering Rick's channel, but then he lowered himself full length along Rick's body, on top of him, and the vampire's black cloak hid what was happening underneath it for some minutes, although the action was obvious. The cloak was rising and falling at the level of the vampire's hips and Rick was crying out and grunting and groaning with each fall of the cloak, making quite clear that the vampire was stroking his channel deep.

A burst of wind flowed through the cemetery and the vampire deftly unclasped the cloak at his neck and let it flutter aside, dramatically, onto the ground beside the tomb, bringing the voyeur cameras directly into the action. Showing Rick still writhing under the vampire, fighting him, but fully embraced and skewered and with no hope of success of escape.

The vampire lowered his mouth onto Rick's chest, and Rick cried out as the vampire's sharp teeth bit into his skin. There were long, red welt marks across Rick's chest and belly and thighs and buttocks from the vampire's sharp fingernails.

The vampire returned his mouth to the hollow of Rick's neck on one side, and Rick screamed a scream caught eerily on the breeze and echoing off the surrounding tomb walls, as the vampire's sharp canines proved to be real and purposeful.

And thirsty.

The cameras panned in closely to capture the panicked, pained look on Rick's face as the teeth punctured the surface of Rick's throat, and a thin line of blood started flowing down from his neck.

Rick fought harder than before, which forced the vampire's cock deeper inside him. The vampire's mouth was making snuffling, slurping sounds at Rick's neck, and, as if the ingestion of whatever blood it could get there increased the vampire's strength, it began to pump Rick's channel harder and quicker.

At the same time, Rick was becoming weaker and weaker. His struggling slowed down, his legs bowed to the side, giving the vampire deeper purchase inside him. He stopped rattling the chains and his head lolled to one side. His breathing was shallower and he began to hear a buzzing in his ears and his eyes were glazing over. Weaker and weaker.

And then Groton was there, warning that it sounded like someone had entered the cemetery. He and Roger were scrabbling at the chain connections, and the vampire disappeared in a hiss and a swirl of mist.

When Rick awoke, totally exhausted, disoriented, and hurting from several slashings on his body, it took him several minutes to realize—signaled first by the snoring—that he had been bathed and was back in the hotelier's bedroom in the Barracks Street hotel.

Near dawn, the hotelier woke, rested, and wanting another fuck for the price of his currently precious rooms. He tried to rouse Rick, but with little luck. So he got out of bed and hauled Rick bodily across the room to where there was a settee and two upholstered chairs. He draped Rick, belly down, over the back of one of the chairs and then fucked his limp body from behind.

Rick didn't even know what was happening.

When he next woke, he was laying across the backseat of the Saab. Groton was driving and Billy Dan was in the passenger seat.

He groaned and tried to sit up, but was unable to do so.

"So, awake at last, are you?" Groton called out cheerily from the front seat as he looked into the back through the rearview mirror. "Maybe you'd best not try to sit up for a while. You were magnificent last night. We got great film. That will be a scene everyone remembers."

"What? Where?" Rick murmured weakly.

"Next stop Dallas," Groton said. "And don't worry. You'll be able to rest and recuperate there. I couldn't find anything but regular hotel rooms, so you'll have no one to bother you all day but maybe a maid who can't read a 'don't disturb' sign."

"Dallas? Rest?" Rick muttered stupidly.

"Dallas is Billy's fantasy, not yours, Rick. You've got a day off."

Oh, yeah, Rick remembered. The cityscape fantasy. On the roof of a city building. That was Billy Dan's chosen scene.

Rick was virtually carried into the hotel room and set to soaking in the tub until the others had to go downtown. Groton, through his network of acquaintances through the country's close-knit gay community somehow had managed to conjure up satisfactorily hunky men to play the superintendent and the cop and had gotten permission to use the roof of a low-lying building in the middle of the city's skyscrapers.

Rick slept the sleep of the dead all day—panicked whenever he drifted up into consciousness that he was, in fact, dead.

At one point in the afternoon he woke, thinking of Phil, needing Phil. He pulled his duffle bag to him from where it had been thrown on a chair beside the bed and, after much effort and cursing, managed to pull out the slip of paper that Phil had given him with his cell phone number. Rick reached for the telephone on the nightstand and tried, unsuccessfully, to dial through on the number. The telephone dial was all a blur to him in his weakened state. He finally gave up in frustration, laid his head back on his pillow with a sob, and sank quickly into almost drugged sleep.

When he became fully conscious much later that evening after the film crew had returned to the hotel, it was to the sight of Groton sitting on the side of the other double bed in the room, waiting for Billy Dan to shower and come out of the bathroom. The first thing Rick saw was a mean-looking hunting knife that Groton had out of its sheath and was moving in slow circles at eye level, catching the light reflecting off the metal from all angles and clearly enjoying the experience. Next to him on the bed was an assortment of different anal toys—dildos of different thicknesses, lengths, and colors; teardrop shaped butt plugs, also of different sizes; and a string of graduated balls.

Rick came up on his elbows in panic—still mentally back on top of the tomb.

"Go back to sleep, Rick," Groton said in a low voice as he resheathed the hunting knife and placed it, almost reverently, on the nightstand between the two beds. "None of this is for you. I have told Lefty Billy will be trained before I return him. We will be busy tonight."

Rick did go back to sleep, but he wasn't totally unconscious. He heard all of the groaning and grunting and crying Billy Dan did in response to his "training" that night. But this was the best of what Rick dreamed and what went through his mind during that night before they left for Amarillo, Texas, on the ongoing journey to Mirage and the film festival.

His dream was horrific—of Groton taking him, not Billy Dan, and using the knife as a dildo as well, slicing Rick up inside, an image undoubtedly surfacing because of the sharp fingernails Rick had endured from the vampire in his own channel. He dreamed of Groton telling Rick that he no longer was of any use to him and that Groton didn't want him ever making movies for anyone else. Rick only assumed the knife was working inside him. Since it was a dream, the sequences were all hazy and nonsensical and he felt no pain at all—at least from the dream. But the sweat and fear it pulled out of him when he woke were quite real.

This led, as he briefly came back to consciousness in the middle of the night to hear nothing but soft moaning from the other bed and Groton's quiet snoring, to reliving the sequence on the tomb in the New Orleans cemetery. Was someone really coming? Was that what led Groton to stop the assault—seemingly in the nick of time? Or had Groton preplanned the cut-off point and had the scene completely under control? Or, worst of all, did Groton intend to let it go to termination—Rick's termination? A snuff movie. Increasingly, Rick was being moved to the side and Billy Dan was being brought into the footlights on this movie. Was Groton, in fact, orchestrating a snuff film as a means to ease Rick out of the movie and out of life? If so, he certainly knew how to make money out of his opportunities. Rick instinctively knew that a snuff film would sell for far more than a Mirage film festival winner would.

Whatever the case, Rick knew he couldn't just drift along any longer—that increasingly his very life was being endangered. There no longer was anyone around him that he could trust. And no one from his old life had a clue where he was. He could disappear off the face of the earth and no one would know what happened to him. Worse, probably no one would care. Then the visage of Phil floated across his mind. Perhaps there was someone who would care after all.

Chapter Eleven: Amarillo

It was another long day of driving over mostly flat and undistinguished and dusty landscape from Dallas to Amarillo, Texas. Driving through the town and almost to Cimarron, the convoy of two vehicles turned south onto a dirt road under a log archway with "The Big C Ranch" engraved on a plaque overhead and drove three more miles until they came upon a long, low ranch house building made out of logs, with a porch running across its entire front. The porch was supported on log posts and the wood railings had wagon wheels set in them. There was a courtyard in back with a double row of rust-splattered white trailers fanning out in a semicircle three quarters of the way around on the east side. There were three evenly spaced doors in the largely identical thirty-foot trailers. On the west side of the semicircle were two rows of carports under one roof. Canvas hangings functioned as doors of each carport space, seemingly to protect the cars from the harsh elements out on this dusty plain—but were, as Rick soon surmised, more accurately present to guard the cars and their license plate numbers from curious eyes.

Coming out onto the porch of the log house to greet them was a near duplicate of the Lefty they had encountered back in the Virginia foothills of the Blue Ridge. He was dressed like an old West card shark, and, Rick guessed, probably was the modern-day equivalent.

"Welcome, welcome. Glad to accommodate you," he bellowed out to Groton as Groton swung the Saab around abreast of the porch in the front car turnabout. "Great idea; hope you win; and, yes, I'd be appreciative of the listing of the ranch in the credits. Make sure it reads 'Gentleman's Gentleman Ranch,' please."

"Ah, yes, nice, very nice indeed. Which one?" he was saying as Groton, Billy Dan, and Rick unfolded themselves from the Saab. The Dodge Truck was just coming up the drive, announcing its arrival by raising a long dust plume behind it.

Groton pointed to Rick, and the card shark, who was being introduced as Sam Easton, the proprietor of the Big C gentleman's gentleman ranch, repeated, "Very nice indeed. Yes, this will be fine." Other men had come out onto the porch to see the arrival. All of them were good looking and well built. There was an assortment of large and small, white and Hispanic and Native American—with one black—and light and dark, bald and hirsute.

One stringy, thirtyish guy broke out of the pack as they exited the front door and walked, bowlegged and none too steady toward the carports, where he lifted a canvas hanging and drove a red Ford 150 pickup out and down the drive toward the main highway. The truck swerved from one side of the road to the other, and Rick murmured a little blessing that they hadn't met this guy on the road on their way in.

After introductions, with Easton pointing out to Groton three particularly burly and hirsute, dark-haired men standing off to the side and then a tall, lanky American Indian in the group of men nearer the door for approval, which Groton provided, Easton said, "You can put your vehicles in any available slot. You can use the third trailer from the left, front row, out back. There are three compartments and you can divvy up beds and work space as you like. I'll show Rick here around inside the main house."

In the main building, Easton's tour of the rooms, most set up for public entertainment, card playing, and deal making—the more private business going on in the trailers behind—stopped behind his office, where his private studio apartment was located.

The bed was a brass one, and, after stripping and examining Rick like he was a horse on the sales block, Easton laid him down on his belly on the bed, tied his wrists over his head to the headboard, spread Rick's butt cheeks with strong, callused hands, and tongued his ass until Rick writhed and moaned—and until Rick begged for the fuck.

Easton knew all of the cocking techniques and put them to lustful and prolonged effect. The mattress was lumpy and the bed creaked and groaned as Easton straddled Rick's hips and rode his ass. But the bed endured—as did Rick.

Groton was lost to them after supper, and, since he was still in the third compartment, unshaved and disheveled and working on his laptop in the morning when Rick came back to the trailers, Rick assumed Groton had worked on his notes and video trimming and reediting throughout the night.

After dinner, which was after Easton released Rick from his bed, Rick had gone to take a look at the trailers. Groton was pounding away on his laptop in the trailer cubicle to the right and Rick didn't do more than check him out and then he closed the door and backed away. Roger was in the middle cubicle, which had a single bed and a cot in it, checking over and adjusting the video equipment.

Rick heard the sounds in the left cubicle before he opened the door. But he opened it anyway. There was a three-quarters bed in there, where presumably Groton and Billy Dan were supposed to sleep—which immediately alerted Rick to the reality that he himself, once again, had been part of the compensation for the accommodations arrangement and had never been slated to sleep in the trailer.

Howard was on his back, naked, on the bed and Billy Dan was riding his cock with abandon and glee.

So much, Rick thought, about any man being a safe choice for cameraman in Groton's crew. But then, Rick mused, that was Groton's problem. Rick was faced with enough of his own problems.

Rick went into the middle compartment. He asked Roger if he wanted to fuck, having a certain nasty streak running through him on sticking it to Groton yet more. Roger said he'd love to, but he'd learned his lesson with the others. He wanted to stick with this job to Mirage.

"Maybe after the showing in Mirage?" he asked hopefully. "It's not like I wouldn't like to have a piece of that sweet ass of yours."

"Yeah, maybe," Rick answered, being aware for the first time that he had no intention of arriving in Mirage. As soon as he could get hold of Phil, he planned to be out of here. "Well, what about a game of Black Jack then?"

"You got it. Just as soon as I get this camera back together."

By the time he had, Howard was back in the room, glowing but looking sheepish too. And that's where the three of them were, in the middle compartment, playing poker— until one of the hunky guys came looking for Rick.

"Boss would like you over at the ranch house," he said.

"Soon as I finished this hand," Rick answered.

"Don't make it too long," the man said and then he was gone. "Boss don't like to wait on anybody."

When Rick entered the ranch house, the entertainment was in full swing. He didn't see the three hirsute men that had been pointed out earlier in the afternoon, but otherwise at least half the men who'd been on the porch when they arrived were there—with a handful of obvious customers. Rick had seen the sets of tires under the gap below most of the canvas hangings in the car ports as he came to the ranch house, and some of the trailers out back seemed to be almost rocking off their foundations, so he had little question where the rest of the "gentlemen's gentlemen" were.

The music was loud and the voices set at high babble level. So Rick was sure that no one could hear him cry out and moan and groan or the raspy creaking of the brass bed in the back corner of the log building where, throughout the night, Easton showed him why his was the number one cock at the Big C. Rick loved being bound and being taken so fully, often, and masterfully.

There was a bit of a set-to the next morning when it was discovered that Billy Dan had left the trailer in the late evening and come into the ranch house and run through most of the tops that had been there. But after Groton had made Billy Dan hand over all of the money he'd been given to Easton and Groton had produced doctor's notes showing that his two boys were clean and had been checked regularly while on the road, Easton simmered down. Groton then laughed and politely—but after some thought, Rick noticed—turned down Easton's offer to buy both Billy Dan and Rick.

* * * *

Groton walked his film group out to a grove of cottonwoods running along a stream not far from the Big C ranch house early the following afternoon. Rick was surprised to see that the cameramen had been augmented by a couple of the guys from the ranch who Groton must have enlisted to help. Rick wondered why the extra cameramen were needed.

He asked Groton.

"We're filming two scenes."

That explained, Rick thought, why both he and Billy Dan had been costumed out in Western-style clothes.

As Groton separated the cameramen out in two groups, Roger and a guy from the ranch being told to go stand by Rick and Groton himself moving with Howard and another guy from the ranch over by Billy Dan, Rick spied a group of the Native American ranch guys coming over from the main house. They were dressed minimally as glorified Indian warriors, in war paint and loin cloths and moccasins and not much of anything else.

Roger started herding Rick and the other cameraman back toward the ranch house, as the Indian "braves" arrived and, at Groton's instruction, began circling Billy Dan menacingly. Groton positioned his cameramen at angles around the group and, as they raised their cameras, the stripping and gangbanging of Billy Dan began. In contrast to what Rick remembered of Billy Dan's dream of this scenario, the Indian warriors were taking turns fucking Billy Dan.

Rick and Roger watched for a while and then Roger nudged Rick toward the back of the ranch house. At the corner of the ranch house, Rick turned to see the tall, rangy Native American Easton had pointed to on the porch the previous day, ride into the cottonwood grove on a saddle-less pinto horse. The warrior was decked out in full TV Indian regalia—except there were only the moccasins and the war paint. He had a magnificently upcurved erection, which the group of Indians swarming around Billy Dan sheathed by lifting Billy Dan up on the horse in front of the Indian brave and lowering his channel to where the erection disappeared from view. As Groton and Howard boarded a jeep being driven by the local cameraman, the Indian brave turned toward the open range in a trot of his horse and already had Billy Dan bouncing up and down on his skewering cock.

And then they were off, the Indian warrior and his sheathing captive white man, galloping across the range, with a jeep and cameramen driving alongside, cameras pointed at Billy Dan's fantasy of an exotic fuck.

Roger's hand went to Rick's sleeve and he turned and followed the cameraman toward a building beyond the trailers. It was a squat building of some thirty by thirty foot dimensions, made out of logs, like the main ranch house.

The three burly hirsute men Easton had pointed out the previous day were standing by the door into the building. Rick couldn't see any windows.

"What's that building?" Rick asked.

"The bathhouse."

That was all he needed to hear. He almost had forgotten that fantasy he had spun for Groton—the last one he'd told the man. In fact, Groton had stopped, before they reached New Orleans, trying to masturbate any fantasies out of Rick. And, to Rick's knowledge, he hadn't pulled any more out of Billy Dan, either. Evidence, coupled with Groton's frenzied work now with the footage he already had, that they were coming to an end of the collection phase—and, Rick, realized, to the end of his usefulness to Groton.

Inside, the bathhouse was quite modern. There were lockers and shower stalls and a Jacuzzi. And there, in the middle of the room, on a dais, was a large, modern rendition of a claw-footed, high-lipped soaking bathtub. The modern part was that the bathtub was translucent, probably made out of Plexiglas. It was half full of water.

Bringing one of the burly hirsute cowboys forward, Roger said to Rick, "Groton says that you are to strip down now—keep on the boots, the hat, and the red scarf around your neck. When the cameras start to roll, you are to help undress this man, make love to his cock, and then fuck him in that bathtub. Groton wants him underneath you in there and your legs hooked over the side, with your booted feet swinging at the sides of the tub. We'll be able to see what's going on under the water, so make it look good. Got it?"

"Yes, I get it," Rick said. And he did; it had been his fantasy. "But what are the other two guys for?"

"Groton auctioned you off to these local guys. Top bidder got you in the tub first. The other guys get to watch. The next highest bidder gets you in the trailer for an hour and then the last guy for a half hour after that."

"Oh."

As in the fantasy, after helping to undress the standing burly cowboy with his hands and lips, Rick sank to his knees in front of him and, for the cameras, made love to the guy's cock with his mouth while he was running his hands over the curly black hair of his barrel chest and hard, man's belly, and his beefy thighs.

When sufficiently aroused, the man lifted and carried Rick over to the tub. He got in first and settled back against one side. Then he lifted Rick, Rick being careful to drape his booted legs over the side of the tub, and settled Rick on his cock, Rick's back against the opposite end of the tub. Taking a lighted cigar in one hand and reaching for Rick's cock with the other, the man, in ten-gallon hat and blue scarf to mirror Rick, began to puff smugly on his cigar and to send the water moving in waves by the upward thrusts of his cock inside Rick's channel.

Later, the third hirsute cowboy overstayed his time with an exhausted Rick by a half-hour, but he paid the extra—as did the first guy who wanted Rick again, this time belly down on a bench in the bathhouse.

That night they locked Billy Dan into Groton's cubicle, but Groton made the mistake of giving Howard the key, and, as far as Rick could discern, Groton spent the night with his laptop in the third cubicle. There was a single bed in there, though, so as far as Rick knew, he did get some sleep. Groton must have been deeply engrossed in his film editing, Rick thought, because Billy Dan and Howard were making quite a bit of noise in their fucking even before Rick had returned to the ranch house.

Rick got little sleep. Sam Easton hadn't gotten any fucking all day, like Rick had. So that night Sam Easton was fresh for it, and, once again, the old brass bed in his room was creaking and bumping up against the log wall throughout the night.

The next day, Groton came to breakfast looking disheveled and red eyed, Roger came from one of the other trailers looking quite satisfied, Billy Dan came in looking sleek and well cared for—which caused Groton to raise an eyebrow and take a long, sweeping, scarching look around the dining room—to no apparent result. Howard stumbled in looking confused and sloppy grinned, and Rick was barely able to drag himself to a chair and heavily lower himself into it, unable to fully close his legs.

Of all of them, Rick looked the most disgruntled. This wasn't because of Easton. Easton had taken good care of Rick in the night. Rick felt whatever itch he had of that kind had been effectively and fully scratched. Rick was unhappy, though, because his scheme was to use one of the telephones in the ranch house and call Phil to come get him. But when Rick had gone to find the scrap of paper Phil's cell phone number was written on, he couldn't find it among his things. He decided that the last time he had tried to use it, when he was zoned out from the meeting with the vampire, he'd dropped the number in the bed sheets at the Dallas hotel and hadn't retrieved it.

Now he wasn't sure what to do. By the end of the meal, however, he was resolved to cut off from Groton right here and now. He obviously wasn't needed by Groton anymore and there was no telling what the man would do to him from here on out. Obviously, Groton was using him as man candy in any way that served Groton's purposes. And Groton hadn't cocked him with that superlong dick for several days. The longer Rick went without that, the easier it was to resist doing what Groton demanded.

He accosted Groton in front of everyone in the dining room, pointing out the he'd done three men in the tub after an auction and hadn't seen any of the money. He wanted some of what he'd earned, right now, and more than just chickenfeed; he'd seen how much had exchanged hands the day before. Groton opened his mouth to retort but then for some reason he thought better of it and pulled out his wallet and counted out ten hundred-dollar bills and handed them to Rick and told him to sit down and shut up now.

While the others were finishing up their breakfasts, Rick excused himself to go to the can. He went to Easton's room and picked up his duffle bag. Then he went out one of the back doors of the ranch house and walked swiftly to the cottonwood tree grove and hid there from view—and watched the front of the ranch house.

In time, the cars were brought out to the front and loaded. There seemed to be some effort to find Rick—but not much. And then after Rick saw Groton and Easton talking and Easton going into the ranch house and coming back out and handing a pile of cash to Groton, all search efforts stopped.

So, that was it, Rick thought. Groton had given him the money so easily because he felt a bit guilty. He'd already decided to sell Rick to the ranch, and he wanted to leave thinking he'd done right by Rick.

Within minutes the Saab and Dodge truck were raising dust as they drove toward the highway from the ranch house. Rick was free. Just like that.

Or so he thought.

He was standing from his crouch in the cottonwoods when hands grabbed at his arms from both sides. He had been found by two of Easton's ranch boys.

"Mr. Easton wants to see you inside," one said in a voice not to be questioned.

"It's OK," Rick said. "I'm going. I'll leave the ranch on my own."

"I don't think so," the other one answered in a gruff voice. "Easton's bought and paid for you. I dare say you're going to be doing what the rest of us do here from now on—at least until you get old and out of shape enough that no one wants to pay for your ass."

Chapter Twelve: Desert Highway

Easton kept Rick in his bed for nearly a week. Then, having assessed Rick's worth in the marketplace and determined the range of what he could give satisfaction for, Easton unceremoniously moved Rick to one of the cubicles in the trailers and, appropriately dressed and indoctrinated in the rules and procedures, Rick was sent into the entertainment rooms of the ranch house. Thereafter Easton didn't touch him again; by then he had a new recruit to break in.

The morning after the first pay-day Friday night that Rick was in the "gentleman's gentleman" pool, Rick came to Easton with a request to be released.

"You want to be released from your contract?"

"What contract?" Rick asked. "I didn't sign any contract."

"I paid good money for you. You want out, buy up your contract."

"How much?"

"Well, let's see, I reckon $5,000 would be about right for a handsome young thing like you with a sweet ass and a taste for it."

"$5,000?" Rick said with disgust. "I don't believe you paid Doug Groton anything like that for me—and I wasn't Groton's to sell anyway." Rick had nearly $2,000 accumulated now; he'd figured he could pay out with Easton and still have some cash for the road.

"Training expenses. I couldn't put you right out on the floor in the condition you came in. I put a whole lot of work into you."

"Shit. You put a whole lot of cock in me—and I didn't hear you complainin' or callin' it work. And you should have paid *me* $5,000 to take it."

"I don't like your attitude much, son," Easton growled, his tone becoming quite menacing. "And as for leaving here, I think I just might let you get a taste of who will come after you if you try." He stood and bellowed, "Melvin, get on in here."

Then he turned to Rick and hissed, "Melvin's been wanting a piece of you for weeks. Time I stopped holding him back."

The club's bouncer, a big bruiser and ugly as sin, his face having been rearranged one too many times in a bar fight, swaggered into the room, a big smile on his face. Rick got the impression this scene had played out a couple of times before.

"Rick here's all yours for the afternoon, Mel. He needs to be serviceable for next Friday night—but have fun. I'd like him brought down about two notches in attitude, please."

Rick turned to flee out of the door, but Mel was between him and his goal. A vicious backhanded swipe to the face sent Rick reeling back and to the side, but a steel grip closed over his wrist and Mel's other fist connected with Rick's midsection, bending him toward the floor with a sound of retching. Clenched fists hit him in the small of his back and Rick went down on the floor.

"No blood or puke in here, please," Easton said. "Take him to his trailer. You know which one it is. Try not to rock the trailer off its foundation." Last thing Rick heard as he was being carried out was Easton laughing at his own joke.

Rick came to in the trailer again as a naked Melvin was pulling his clothes off. Rick made a drunken lunge for the door, but Melvin's hand spun him around and Melvin's other fist caught him under the chin.

A dazed and moaning Rick was loose as a rag doll and bent over at the waist, Melvin's arms locked under his waist, and Rick's body just bouncing around, feet off the floor, at the whim of Melvin's cocking, as, standing and holding Rick's hips to his crotch, the bouncer administered Rick's first punishing fuck of a long afternoon.

The next Saturday morning in the predawn, the ranch having quieted down from a raucous pay-day Friday celebration, Rick quietly gathered the few things he had together in his duffel bag and, as silently as he could, limped out of the compound and down the three miles to the end of the drive into the Big C ranch.

At the intersection with the highway, he looked east and west, not sure of where he wanted to go. The past—where he'd come from, in the east—didn't seem to hold any promise for him. So, he turned the toes of his cowboy boots toward the west and started walking down the side of the highway in dusty, desolated northwest Texas.

For the first ten miles of his walk, Rick started at sound of any approaching vehicle from the direction of the Big C ranch, and in this empty space he could hear an engine noise more than a mile away. When he heard the rare approaching car, he went into the drainage ditch at the side of the road. But nothing driving by appeared to be from the ranch. After a while, Rick decided Easton had been bluffing about coming after him. In a strange way, he was disappointed. Rick couldn't think of anyone—with the possible exception of Phil—who shed a tear or gave a damn about him moving on.

* * * *

Once the sun came up, Rick began to realize what a dumb idea it was just to be walking out on the side of a Texas dual-lane highway under the blazing Texas sun.

He hadn't even brought any water with him, and he was still bruised and, he suspected, didn't have everything inside him in its right place from the working over Melvin had given him the week before. He was limping and couldn't even stand up straight as he walked because of a pain in his side that had been there for a week. He had had to service three customers the previous night and all of them had been focused on dipping their own cocks, so he felt worse now than he had Friday morning.

And as he walked, he reviewed his circumstances. And the hotter he became and the more thirsty and the more shuffling rather than walking, the more depressed he became. The fight for life was slowly ebbing away.

Cars passed him—but at high speed. None stopped. And each time one passed, Rick took another, more distant, step from the margin of the highway, trying to escape the choking dust their wheels threw up in his face.

He didn't even realize it when he stopped putting one foot in front of another and simply stood and shuddered for a brief time, before sinking down into the desert sand a good twenty feet from the side of the road.

Sometime later, Rick heard the sound of gravel on tires and lifted his head enough to see an old, rusty sedan from the sixties or seventies pulling over to the side of the road just past where he was lying. He groaned and rolled over onto his side.

"Water . . . please," he whispered through parched lips as three Hispanic men approached him cautiously.

But they didn't offer water or any other form of respite. And if any of them said a word, it was not loud enough for Rick to hear. One of them, with a face of indeterminate age, lined with years of weariness and backbreaking scrabbling for hard-fought existence, crouched down beside him, watching him intently for signs of objection or resistance, while the other two pawed through his duffel bag, taking whatever appealed to them, animated and thrilled when they came upon his stash of cash. The last sound Rick heard as he groaned and drifted off into a haze was the sound of doors slamming and gravel being thrown up by the tires of a departing car.

Chapter Thirteen: Santa Fe

The cook had fed us with steak and cleaned up and left, leaving the two of us alone. My host put some soft music on and lit the fire. The wine had been excellent and I was feeling it in my head. The white bear-skin rug in front of the fire looked so inviting, and I wanted my head to stop spinning, so I laid down on that on my belly, facing the fire, staring into it and becoming quite mellow. My host left me there for a short time, letting the fire and the music and the soft rug and the buzz from the wine float me away.

He was back, in a short cotton robe. He must have been at least in his late forties or early fifties, but he'd aged well. His leg muscles were firm and I thought that he must have been an athlete at one time—and probably still worked out. As he leaned down to me, the front of the cotton robe opened and I saw a well-developed chest with a matting of salt-and-pepper curly hair running from his chest down in a thin line to where the lapels of the robe met.

"Some port or cognac?" he asked in a rich baritone. His face was distinguished. A lawyer or a banker or corporate CEO. Even after two weeks, I didn't know. He spoke little about himself, showing more concern for me. So kind. If he hadn't found me at the side of the desert highway, brought me to this big house on the ridge above Santa Fe, and had a doctor in to look at me after what the beating and the hours on the sand by the highway had done to me . . .

The steel gray hair was expertly cut, a perfect-teeth smile. A slight scar under his left eye—his eyes were hazel and so alive—only served to emphasize how handsome his chiseled features were. Model handsome. A healthy Santa Fe tan smoothed out the laugh-line wrinkles.

"No thanks, Mr. Grimes. Another drop of alcohol and I'd go right to sleep."

"We couldn't have that, now, could we?" he answered, the low laugh conveying his mood. "And I've told you, it's Bill."

"I have trouble with that . . . Bill. You've been so kind, and there's such a divide between us."

"We must see what we can do about that too. Here, take a look at these. I work with photography. I'd like to know what you think."

He was handing a folder to me. I opened the cover to find a set of loose photographs. The ones on top were art shots—nudes—of a young, handsome youth. A bit younger than me. About nineteen, I'd guess. The photos were expertly done, although it wasn't the artistry of them that took my attention. Toward the bottom of the pile, the photographs were more explicit—much more explicit as I leafed through to the bottom of the stack. And the youth wasn't alone. Grimes too was in these photos. I turned my head toward the sofa to see the cotton robe fall onto it in folds.

I shuddered and stiffened as his body came down on top of me, covering me full length. My torso was raised on my elbows, as I was fanning through the photographs. His hands laced in underneath me and he was unbuttoning my shirt and then pulling it off my arms.

"Relax," he whispered in my ears. "Just concentrate on the photos and let your body drift with me."

I did what I could to let the tension in my body flow away. "Mr. Grimes. Bill," I whispered.

"Sure you don't want to try the Cognac? I still have the taste of it in my mouth," he whispered back at me. He cupped my chin and turned my face toward his, and, when he kissed me, I tasted the rich, full-bodied nectar of the wine.

His hips were moving against my pelvis, and I felt the hardness of him through the material of my jeans and briefs.

I felt the palm of a hand on my belly and fingers working at the buttons of my jeans. Instinctively, without conscious control, I lifted my butt into his crotch as the zipper of my jeans was being pulled down. I wanted him to know there would be no struggle, no indecision, no holding back for whatever he wanted. He had paid for this in full. All of the hardness went out of my jaw and I opened my mouth totally to him.

The moaning I heard was almost detached, but I recognized it as mine.

He wouldn't release the hold of his lips on mine and in the wake of the taste of the cognac, his tongue had invaded my mouth cavity. I could hardly breath. But I didn't care if I couldn't. He was still possessing my mouth as he was pulling my jeans and briefs below my hips.

Skin on skin now below the belly. A hard dick inside my butt crack, stroking up and down on the rim of my hole. I shuddered and groaned and he released my mouth and gave a low, comfortable laugh.

"The photos. Concentrate on the photos," he said.

I returned my attention to the photographs, pushing through the ones of the handsome youth solo, down to the ones of the youth with Grimes. He was moving down the line of my back now. Kissing and licking my shoulder blades, while one hand pulled my jeans and briefs down and off my legs and the other one worked my nipples and then came down to palm my belly as his lips reached the mounds of my butt cheeks.

His teeth nipped at the sensitive skin of my rump and I groaned as I heard the low, appreciative laugh again. I felt a light slap on each cheek and they were being squeezed and nipped again. A hand went between my thighs and pulled my cock and balls through. I tried to widen my stance, but he moved his forearms to trap my thighs close together, tightly against my dick. A hand possessed my cock and slowly stroked down.

"Bill, Bill," I whispered.

"Ah the divide narrows, doesn't it? Surely there will be no trouble with first names now," he answered back. And then that arousing laugh again. He clearly was enjoying this.

"Do you like the photos?" he asked. "Don't the two of us make the smashing pair?"

"Yes." It was a whisper.

"Does the lad look happy? Am I fucking him well?"

"Yes." It was a whimper, followed with a moan.

He had taken both hands and was spreading and squeezing my butt cheeks with them. When he blew across my hole, I shivered and groaned.

"So nice. Such a rosy bud. And already opening."

"Bill," I whispered. "Bill." And then "Bill!" as he kissed the hole and his tongue started working into me. I writhed under him for countless minutes as he tongued my hole and worked my cock with his hand. Intermittently he moved his mouth down to my cock and balls and gave suck, and during these intervals his fingers invaded my channel and found my prostate.

"Bill, Bill! I'm gonna come. You're gonna make me—"

"Oh, I hope so, Rick," he muttered. "I certainly hope so." And then he laughed again.

And I came.

He covered my back fully with his body again and his cock was rubbing inside my cheeks once more. I raised my pelvis to him. Presenting to him. Wanting him. Wanting him to know I wanted him. "Bill," I whined.

"Ah, are you ready? Do you want me inside you? Permission to fuck, my young lad? Jeff wants his daddy?"

"Yes," I whimpered, all of my senses focused on the shaft rubbing across my hole, not even catching the reference to a Jeff.

He went up on his knees, reaching over to the sofa. I heard the slight rustle of the condom packet as he opened it, and then I felt the coldness of the lubricant he poured liberally between my cheeks and worked into my opening with probing fingers. My chest was flat on the floor, my cheek against the photos of Grimes fucking the youth, my arms splayed out at my side. I was up on my knees, though, with my quivering butt raised to him, my legs spread.

Fuck me, fuck me now, was what I was trying to convey.

He crouched over me, pulling my chest up, me now on all fours. The cock was rubbing inside my crack again, sending electric impulses as it stroked again and again against my hole.

"Please. Bill, Please!" I begged.

He laughed. And then I felt the bulb presented at my hole and he was slowly pushing into me. I gasped and my eyes started to water and both my elbows and my knees began to quiver and to give way. But Bill, crouched over my midsection and continuing to enter me, held me up with strong arms wrapped under my rib cage. I felt his lips at my cheeks, and I turned my face to him, letting him possess my mouth again—masking my groans and moans.

Who would have known he was so thick and hard—and that it would take so much length of my channel for him to bottom?

Coming out of the kiss, my face was suspended over the photographs. The one on top was of Grimes crouched over the hips of the young man, who was on all fours—on a white bear-skin rug in front of a fireplace; this fireplace. The expression on the young man's face was one of ecstasy. Bill was looking into the camera with an expression that almost conveyed, "At last; in at last."

Only half hidden below that was a photo of the young man on his back on the same furry rug and Grimes kneeling between his thighs, knees under and raising the young man's buttocks, Grimes fisting the youth's slim ankles and holding his legs up and out, wide. I could see a good two inches of the root of a thick cock at the young man's channel opening. And again, that "gone to paradise" expression on the young man's face.

A third photo was of Grimes completely sheathed, the youth's legs running up Grimes's torso now, his hands reaching around Grime's thick waist and clutching the older man's thin butt cheeks close to him with fingers digging into the flesh, obviously trying to take in every centimeter of the cock. Eyes wild, mouth gaping open, and tongue hanging out. I trembled in anticipation.

He stroked me so long and hard that my elbows and knees did give out and, with a laugh, he rode me to the rug and kept on riding. He was babbling as he fucked me, and I occasionally heard the name "Jeff" spoken. But never the name "Rick."

Fucking me at such depth, and so filling. My channel walls undulating across the shaft as it mastered me. Throbbing, hot, relentless. Strong hands pulling my thighs in tight. Oh, god, the tightness. The almost despair as he pulls back. Oh, no, don't leave me! Oh, shit, yes! at the long hard plunge back to the depths. Yes! Again. Oh, yes! And again. Oh Shit! And AGAIN. Paradise. Faster now—stroke, stroke, hold, stroke—making me pant and writhe against his strong hands and moan—and beg for it to go on and on.

I felt him tighten and take in a long breath and then—with my channel trying, unsuccessfully, to close on his cock and keep him inside me—he pulled out of me, and I groaned at the loss of him and heard the condom being ripped away and then felt the flow of him on the small of my back.

He covered my back with his torso again and continued moving on top of me, stroking the small of my back with his cock through his cum. He hands glided along my arms and took my wrists. I turned my lips to him again. His prisoner for as long as he wanted.

"I'm sorry if you weren't expecting that this evening," he whispered in my ear when he once more let loose of my lips.

"I don't know what took you so long," I answered, with a sigh.

"I thought perhaps I assumed so much. But you are so beautiful and sexy. I couldn't help myself. Hardly a good host."

"You saved my life," I whispered back. "And . . . and the perfect host. Almost too polite, I was beginning to think."

He turned me on my back, my head resting in the pile of his photographs. He covered my body with his, his cock lying against my own between our still-heaving bellies. I looked down the line of his body. His barrel chest with the matting of salt-and-pepper gray standing out in moist curls and below that a still-flat, hard belly—even at his age. I wanted to run my hands through the matting on his chest, to search out the taut nipples I saw hiding there between the curls of the hair. But he had his fists wrapped around my wrists and they were trapped on either side of my shoulders. So, instead, I dipped and raised my face into his chest. I found a nipple almost immediately and sucked it in hard as he gasped and then I nipped at it, which produced a yelp from his mouth and an engorging surge in his cock.

Releasing one of my wrists, his hand grabbed my head under the chin and forced it back into the pile of photographs and his mouth was hungrily attacking mine, his tongue invading, every bit as filling and probing as his cock had been. I gasped and nearly gagged.

I wrapped my legs around his, my heels rubbing up and down his hard calves. His free hand snaked between our bellies before I could completely push in as close as I could to every inch of him. The hand wrapped our two cocks together. And he stroked our shafts and worked my mouth with his until, with a lurch and a shudder, I came again.

He released my mouth and cock then. I could feel he was fully hard again. Amazing for his age. Not so much, though, considering the strength and power of his fuck. He raised his torso off mine a bit and looked down into my eyes. He was smiling that melting smile of his—the one I saw in the photographs when it was clear that he had mastered the young man to exhaustion.

"That's not fair," he said in a tone of false pout. "You've gone twice and I only once. Would you mind terribly if—?"

"I hoped you would," I whispered breathlessly, my mind possessed by what I'd seen in the photographs, as he knelt between my legs, pulled my buttocks up on top of his thighs, and reached over on the sofa for another condom packet. I lifted one of my legs up his torso to hook an ankle on his right shoulder while I watched him roll the condom on his cock and prepared to raise the other to his left shoulder when he was crowned, positioning myself to roll up my rump to receive the deepest thrusts I could eke out of him. I spied three more condom packets on the sofa and shivered in anticipation. I had seen other photos of other fuck positions the young man obviously had enjoyed.

But who, I was wondering, who the fuck was Jeff?

* * * *

"Hey, guy, are you OK? Here, here. I brought some water. There, let's get you up and . . . for the love of god, you look just like . . . is it a mirage? There for a second. . . . Here. Yes, drink some of this . . . not too much at first. Later more. Are you OK?"

"K," Rick said. He'd been on his side, curled up, the pain in his side grinding away as the only clue that he was still live. The man turned him onto his butt and raised his torso, supporting him underneath with a strong arm. And he was offering a plastic bottle of commercial water for Rick to sip from.

Rick groaned from the pain in his side when his body was moved, but his hand with the bottle of water was at his lips and he almost had to be restrained from gulping down too much of it.

"Sorry, are you hurt? More than just the heat in the desert?" the man asked.

"Side," Rick answered. "Hurts." He looked up at the man. A handsome businessman type, slim build but good strength. Gray haired. In his forties or fifties. Beyond him, at the side of the road, Rick saw a late-model Mercedes sedan. Not the cheapest model.

The man had lifted Rick's shirt. "It's bruised. Have you been in a fight or something? Are you from around here. Anyone I can call?"

"No one. Just walkin' . . . walkin' to Mirage," Rick said.

"Mirage?" the man said and looked at Rick funny. Rick thought there was something else he was going to say, but then he didn't. "You going east or west?"

"West. Mirage, Arizona," Rick said and then he grimaced and reached for the water bottle. "Sorry. Can I? Mouth feels like cotton."

The Man looked like he understood better. "Ah. Arizona. Got to get through New Mexico first, and you're obviously in the need of a doctor—and to get out of this sun. I see there are other bruises. Someone's worked you over. Yellowing, though, not that recent. Here, I live in Santa Fe. In a bit of a hurry. There aren't any hospitals around here that I know of. I can take you to Santa Fe and have a doctor who I can get to look at you. That OK?"

And then when he saw that Rick wasn't responding. "That OK, son? Oh, lord, don't zone out on me now. I swear the resemblance is . . ."

But Rick wasn't listening. Rick had lost consciousness.

When he regained consciousness, he was lying along the backseat of a luxuriously appointed car. He wondered if this was his chariot to heaven.

"Where? What?" he muttered.

"Oh good, you've come to. I couldn't leave you there out on the desert between nowhere and nowhere else. We're on the way to Santa Fe. But if you want me to leave you somewhere—"

"No, that's . . . that's fine," Rick murmured. "No place better than that. And . . . thanks."

"There's a water bottle on the floor of the car by your head," the man said in a rich baritone that exuded relief. "Just don't try to drink too much too fast. We'll be home in about four hours."

"Perfect," Rick muttered. And although his throat was parched, he drifted back off to sleep, dreaming of a knife cutting into his side. Home, where was home for him? This was Rick's last thought before blacking out.

* * * *

"It's a bruised kidney," the doctor was saying. He was standing over Rick, who was tucked into a queen-sized bed in a rather large room that must have belonged to a young boy, one who had enjoyed athletics and Spider Man, although the Spider Man stuff mostly had drifted to the floor to be replaced by Rock band posters. The baseball and football trophies had obviously held their place of honor, though.

"It's on the mend already. I've seen to some other cuts and bruises that should have been taken care of a week or more ago, but are managing pretty well on their own now. You were in some sort of fist fight, were you?"

"There was something like that, but I never had a chance to get into it."

"I see," the doctor said. "Ganged up on, were you?"

"One was enough."

"I'd say one was more than enough. A relative of Bill's, are you?"

"Bill?"

"Bill Grimes. This is his house. He called me in."

"No. He's just a good Samaritan," Rick answered. "Picked me up on the road outside Amarillo."

"Texas?" the doctor said with surprise.

"Yeah, I guess that's where Amarillo is. I've come from back east."

"Walked the whole way?"

"No. I was with some other guys."

"Guys with bruised fists?"

"No. But it's complicated."

"And now you are here in Bill Grimes's house." It was said like there was some meaning behind it.

"Yeah, I guess. I feel like I've slept forever."

"Bill said you got in late last night. He couldn't get me until this morning. I just got home this morning from Vegas."

The doctor looked at Rick for a long minute before he spoke again. He was putting medical stuff back in his bag and snapped it shut. "And you say you aren't a relative of Bill's?"

"No. He just stopped for me. I was done on the side of the highway."

"I see," the doctor said. That tone again of there being more than just seeing. But then he got up. At the door, he turned and said, "I'll look in at you again tomorrow. Another couple of days, and I think you can get out of bed without much pain."

Only when the doctor was gone did Rick realize he was naked under the sheets—and clean. He blushed, suddenly bringing to mind the only thing he had remembered about arriving here. They've driven up the slopes above old Santa Fe, and Rick had the impression of a long, low adobe building that went on forever. And then an elegant, open space of an entryway with a sunken living room below, beyond which, through a great expansion of glass, the twinkling lights of a low-lying city could be seen. The wall of windows was broken by a gigantic fireplace with a white bear-skin rug in front of it. A large dining area was off to the right upon entering the front door, opening to a similarly large kitchen beyond with gleaming black glass fronts on the appliances. To the left of the door was a corridor leading back to what must be a bedroom wing and an adobe-encased staircase leading to a second floor area above the bedroom wing.

The man who had brought him here in his Mercedes—who Rick only now knew was named Bill Grimes—had half carried Rick to a Leather sofa near the fireplace and gently lowered him down into the corner of that.

"I'll be just a few minutes," he'd said. "I'll prepare a room for you and be right back down. And I'll bring you something that will help with the pain."

The man disappeared up the stairs to the second floor. Rick looked around and it didn't take him long to find out something important about the man who had saved him in the desert. There was considerable art work around. Bronze and silver sculptures and oil paintings. All large and showy, and obviously expensive. The sculptures were all of men's muscled torsos and the paintings were male nudes. There wasn't much more bric-a-brac around except for along the tops of the bookcase balcony rising in a semicircle around the inner side of the living room, separating the sunken area from the corridor and dining room on the raised level. This space was devoted to framed photographs. They were too far away for Rick to see, and his eyes kept going back to the artwork anyway. Two art books lay on the huge, glass-topped coffee table, both with black-and-white photos of artfully posed male nudes on the cover.

When the man returned, he had changed to a short cotton robe and was carrying a glass with fizzing liquid in it. As Rick took this down in several long gulps, the man asked him what his name was, how old he was, and where his family was and, it seemed, told Rick his own name. But none of this stuck—neither the specific questions nor the answers. Almost before Rick had finished drinking the medicine, his eyelids were drooping and he was drifting off to sleep.

The next face Rick saw was the face of the doctor in that room with the posters and the athletic trophies.

After the doctor left, Bill Grimes appeared with a bowl of soup and a glass of milk, and Rick's nearly two-week period began of healing his wounds from his beating at the Big C ranch and his heat stroke from the stumble on foot along the highway out of Amarillo.

Grimes gave Rick plenty of time to rest and sleep and during that time, all conversation, which was terse and relatively rare, was focused on Rick and on making him well.

Grimes said little about himself and Rick didn't press him. For most of the first week, Rick was in a semiconscious state. The doctor only visited three times—covering the first three days. Whatever he left for Rick to take was of such a strong nature that Rick spent more time sleeping and when he was sleeping, he slept as the dead.

Each morning when he came back into a semiconscious state, he was naked and clean under the sheets.

Twelve days after his arrival, Rick made his first journey down the stairs and to the living room. For two days prior to that, he had made sojourns out onto a balcony off the bedroom he was in, the bedroom also having its own full bath and a massive walk-in closet with just two hangars—his neatly cleaned and pressed jeans, cowboy shirt and briefs hanging on one and a cotton robe similar to the one he'd seen Grimes wear on the other. Rick's duffel bag was on the floor. There was very little in the duffel bag; just some clothes. Whatever money Rick had once had was now gone, and it took Rick a few minutes to remember the Hispanic men who had robbed him by the side of the road.

Feeling well enough to move about, Rick put on the cotton robe and went out on the balcony, which was oriented out toward the west and hovered over a steep slope down the ridge side. He shivered when he looked down into the ravine. It must be a drop of five stories or more down to the rocks in the dry stream bed.

When he decided to go down to the living room for the first time, he put on his jeans and cowboy shirt. When he got to the bottom of the stairs, which required some effort as weak as he was, he found a rather rotund Mexican woman in the kitchen cutting up food and humming. She smiled at him and he smiled back. He went to the window by the fireplace in the living room, which turned out to be a French door—all of the space on either side of the fireplace was devoted to the same sort of door—Rick turned the handle, wanting to go out onto the portal beyond and take in the fresh mountain air. The door was locked, as was the one beside it. He didn't see any knob or anything to unlock it from the inside.

He turned to ask the woman in the kitchen about going out onto the portal, but he saw, instead, Bill Grimes walking briskly toward him from a room beyond the kitchen.

"Ah, Rick, it's good you're up and about. Come on back to the den and let's have a drink and I'd like to show you the book of Ansel Adams photographs I was in Dallas buying before we met. Do you know who Ansel Adams is?"

"Yes, I studied him in a photography class," Rick answered.

They entered a room almost as large as the living room. All of the artwork here was of Southwestern art—and most of it consisted of photographs. There were bookcases lining two walls. These cases were packed with art books, most, that Rick could see, of Southwestern landscape oils and lithographs—Georgia O'Keefe type stuff or of landscape photography. One whole section, though, caught Rick's attention. They looked like photographs of male nudes. He started to gravitate toward those, but Grimes took him by the arm and led him toward a leather sofa with a glass-topped coffee table in front of it. A large book was open on the table, and even Rick could see that the photo shown was an Ansel Adams.

"Here, this is the book I wanted to show you. And here's a drink. I'm sure it will be OK for you to drink this now. You're almost fully well, I think."

Rick could tell from the delicate touch of the man's fingers on his arm and from the way he looked into Rick's eyes—the flash in his own hazel eyes, and the curve of his mouth when he smiled—that he wanted Rick. Rick had now been into this sort of thing for quite a few months—going back to Tony, who had given Rick the exact same look before fucking him.

Although the artwork in the living room had alerted Rick, he would have known from how the man touched him and looked at him now that this is what the man wanted. What the artwork had done for Rick, though, was to give him time to think about the circumstances. The fact that the guy had stopped for him and brought him here and gotten a doctor to see him and nursed him. This all made Rick feel like he owed the man something. Beyond that, the man was quite handsome and well built. And overriding everything else, Rick liked to be fucked and hadn't been for two weeks.

Rick would like this Grimes guy to think he was seducing Rick, if that's the way he wanted to play it. But Rick was already prepared. He was ready to play.

Rick started drinking the drink as he sat next to Grimes while Grimes turned the pages of the Ansel Adams book and spoke in that rich baritone of his about this nuance and that of lighting and location and time of day. Rick had no idea when either the drink or the photography show was finished, though, as the strain of a first trip downstairs had gotten to him and he drifted off to sleep.

The next morning he awoke in the room on the second floor. He was clean and naked under the sheets.

The next night, Grimes himself decided that Rick was well and strong enough to come down to the dining room for a full meal. The cook prepared them a delicious steak dinner with excellent wine. As they ate, she cleaned up the kitchen and was gone before they were finished.

Grimes invited Rick to go on down into the living room and to take his wine glass with him. Rick felt hazy from the wine, but it was so good that he took another drink of it at the table. He didn't feel steady enough, though, to carry his glass down into the living room, so he left the glass on the dining room table and carefully negotiated the stairs down there with the use of both hands.

Rick perched on the sofa as Grimes moved about the room, dimming the lights, putting soft music on the CD changer, and lighting the fire.

As Grimes was doing this, Rick looked around, sensing that there was something different about the room than from the time he'd first sat on this sofa two weeks previously. It wasn't the artwork; that was all still in place. Then, he noticed that the photographs were gone. The living room bookcases were now empty of all photographs. In their place were some replicas—or genuine as far as Rick knew—of black and white Southwestern native pottery.

Rick didn't dwell on this find. His head was spinning from the first alcohol he'd drunk since coming here. But that wasn't completely true; he'd had a drink in the den with Grimes the previous afternoon. Of course he hadn't been able to hold that very well either.

He wanted his head to stop spinning. The fire and the bear rug looked so inviting. He slipped down onto the rug on his belly, facing the fire.

Grimes entered from the bedroom wing, dressed in his short cotton robe. He offered Rick some port or cognac to top off the evening, but Rick begged off. Then Grimes was leaning down to Rick, with a portfolio in his hand.

"Here, take a look at these," he said. "I work with photography. I'd like to know what you think."

As Rick fanned the photographs out—artistic nude shots of a young man, and more explicit photos below those in the stack of the young man with Grimes—Rick turned his face to the sofa to see the cotton robe fall onto it in folds.

And then Grimes was lowering his naked body onto Rick's back.

They fucked for an hour and more, in several positions—all inspired by the photographs Grimes dropped on the rug under Rick's face. As the logs in the fireplace were being reduced to glowing embers and Grimes was on his side, with Rick cuddled into his chest and Grimes holding Rick's leg up for access to Rick's channel as he was still stroking him deep in a side split, Grimes put his lips to Rick's ear and said, "It's so nice. You're such a sweet fuck."

"Yes, yes, it is nice," Rick whispered back with a mellow sigh.

"It's so much nicer fucking you when you are conscious," Grimes said.

Rick froze in shock and instant realization. Going out like a light after being given a drink; waking up naked under the sheets and clean—it all fit into place with just that one statement from Grimes. Rick gasped and tightened up and shuddered, marking this as the start of his need to be out of this house, to escape the insane clutches of this man.

If Grimes noticed the change in Rick, he didn't signal it. He just kept on stroking deep inside Rick's channel. And ultimately Rick gave into the fuck fully and lay there panting and moaning, arms and legs spread in full supplication for anything else Grimes would want to do and with a sloppy grin on his face. When Grimes was finished inside him, he withdrew and stood and went to the kitchen for another bottle of wine. He came back into the living room with a photography book on Mapplethorpe nude male models and sat on the sofa, leafing through the pages. At length he looked down at Rick again, still sprawled on the bearskin rug, completely open to him. Grimes smiled and got up from the sofa and went over to a table and retrieved a camera. He came back.

"Don't move. You look lusciously vulnerable and open."

Rick did as he asked, watching Grimes circle him, snapping off shot after shot. This was something Rick was accustomed to; this was of the world Douglas Groton had initiated him into. Gradually, Grimes narrowed in on Rick until he was kneeling between the young man's open thighs.

"You. You do it," he murmured.

Rick reached down and took Grime's reengorged cock in his hands and guided it into his hole, as Grime's fired off camera shot after shot of the entry and then panned up to catch the pain and shock in Rick's eyes as Grimes slammed his cock home deep and immediately began to stroke hard.

* * * *

Rick hadn't thought about escaping Grimes's house nearly fast enough, and the more he just drifted along, the harder thoughts of escape became. The easiest time to try to split and run would have been at the point of learning that Grimes had already been fucking him while he was unconscious—probably from the first night Rick had been here. Thinking on it retrospectively, Rick remembered that the first thing Grimes did when they arrived at the house was to strip and put on one of those skimpy cotton robes of his. He'd then given Rick something to drink that had put him out like a light. There was every reason to believe that Grimes fucked him as soon as he was unconscious—that first night. Most of the reason Rick wasn't quick off the mark was that he loved Grimes's cocking. He loved seeing the photos of what the man was going to do to him—and then having it done—and then, sometimes the photos Grimes took while fucking him. Groton had taught him to love this.

And at the same time he found that escape wasn't going to be easy, he began to see what the rhythm of life was going to be like around here.

Grimes had fucked Rick so silly on the bear-skin rug in front of the fireplace that he let Grimes help him upstairs to his bedroom. While Rick showered, Grimes stripped the bedroom bare of all of Rick's clothes. And when Rick came out of the bathroom, he found he had been locked into the bedroom. So much for a quick exit.

And then, late in the night, Grimes came back into the room and woke Rick in mid fuck. This was a more gentle, loving fucking. Always the taking in other parts of the house was exotic, lustful. But here, in Rick's bedroom, it was slow and attentive to Rick's needs—almost loving. It was this fucking, too, when Grimes dispensed with the use of a condom. It was then, at the height of passion, as his ejaculation started and Rick felt the strong flow of Grimes inside him, that Grimes murmured the name that wasn't Rick's: Jeff. They then settled down to sleep, their bodies entwined. In the morning, Grimes was gone and the door was locked.

He appeared with a breakfast tray.

"I think it best for you to rest up here during the day, Rick," he said. He made no mention of the missing clothes. And believing the man unbalanced and set on a short fuse, Rick said nothing about the missing clothes. He was more concerned that Grimes didn't mention not using a condom the previous night. This gripped Rick like a hand tightening around his throat. This brought a permanence to this ritual of the night that caused the ringing of trap doors shutting in Rick's mind as nothing else had.

"I'll bring you your breakfasts and lunches. The housekeeper will make enough for you to eat a dinner she's prepared after I have done so in the evening, and then you can come down and we'll enjoy ourselves. I have so many interesting photography books to show you—so many ways I want to fuck you."

Rick thought of trying to get to the housekeeper while she was here, but he already knew she only spoke Spanish, and, from the evidence of what he saw that Grimes kept around the house, Rick could only assume that she already knew about Grimes's "arrangements" and perhaps was paid enough to not help Rick even if she could. And then there was the part that Rick could only come into her presence in the nude.

That night, after dark, when Grimes let Rick come downstairs to eat dinner, the first thing that Rick noticed were that two video cameras had been set up—one in the dining room and one in the foyer corridor, that were panned down to the bear-skin rug in the living room.

He knew what these were for. And, strangely, they were more calming than shocking to him. This had been what he had associated with the sex act as Doug Groton had brought him across the country toward Mirage, Arizona. Being on camera would give him a role. He had experience in that.

As Rick ate, wolfing the food down both because it was good and also because fucking taxed so much of his energy and he was being taken multiple times twice a day now, Grimes, in one of the several short cotton robes he had, sat patiently at the table, looking through a book of pornographic male art, showing Rick images Grimes liked or thought that Rick would.

"This is the art of Dan Saba," he said as he turned the book toward Rick. "Can you see the sensuality of it? The time they obviously are taking in his posings? The arousal and love in their eyes?"

"Umm, muh," Rick responded. Yeah, right, it looked like the younger guy was enjoying the older one fucking him. And, yeah, the shot of the young guy leaning back and his legs raised on the bench and spread and giving a good shot of his hole, cock, and balls was pretty good too. And the one of two guys fucking in a shower.

"And here, in this book, Tony Caperton's 'On the Beach'—obviously mimicking that famous pose from the movie. Don't the two lovers look totally taken with each other?"

Grimes was holding the book open with one hand and already stroking Rick's cock with the other.

"Oh, god, yes, I like that painting. It's a lot like the one you have on the wall over in the foyer, isn't it?"

"Yes. You've a good eye. That's by the same artist."

"I think I've eaten enough now," Rick said, as he laid a hand on Grimes's chest and ran his fingers through the curly hair there. His eyes told Grimes that Rick was ready and open to him.

Grimes fucked Rick slowly and sensually on the bear-skin rug, murmuring that Rick should think of the artwork he had seen. All the time the cameras were whirring. The slowness and total taking of the cocking did recall in Rick's mind the artwork.

On successive evenings, the two played wrestlers on the rug for the cameras after the form of a Thomas Eakins painting of that name and Rick was introduced to a psychedelic drug for a wild, full-color and high fantasy taking in the style of Jon Smith. An image of a fucking bent over a table was played out in the dining room and another series of art photos inspired a scene where both just stood in the middle of the

155

living room, and Grimes spiked Rick's ass from behind and wrapped his hands around him and Rick arched back to him and they kissed while Grimes gave Rick a rocking fuck.

A Tom of Finland portfolio moved them on to Rick's wrists being tied to two pillars in the foyer, and Grimes gripping his butt cheeks and standing between Rick's spread legs and swing fucking him roughly.

They even explored Japanese art, where Grimes produced two brocade robes and Rick sat in his lap facing him, and the fuck started inside the robes, with nothing provocative seen other than the knowledge of the movement of their bodies assuring the camera-aided voyeur that they were fucking. And then slowly, ever so slowly Grimes opened up Rick's robe to expose body parts that Grimes would tease with his lips and teeth, until Rick's body was revealed fully at the height of the fuck. The film would be cut to focus in on root of the cock lengthening and shortening as it moved in and out of Rick's hole, surrounded by the folds of the soft brocade of two Japanese robes, ending in a shudder of the cock root marking the ejaculation.

And then once, when it appeared Rick was completely under his spell, Grimes produced the photos of him fucking an unconscious Rick in the shower, often letting the slick tiled wall of the shower support Rick's back while Grimes stood and held Rick's legs around his hips, and pumped up into his channel—or Grimes holding Rick's hips up to his cock, while Rick's shoulders were on the wet tiles of the shower floor and his head resting on a rolled-up, soaked towel, Rick's legs akimbo, and Grimes fucking down into his channel.

"These are of the first time, that first night," Grimes said in a low voice dripping of arousal. "I will always cherish these."

And Grimes wanted to repeat all of that for video cameras on tripods too—adding the effect of a Rick who was actually aware of what was happening to him.

The nights were more private, Grimes making complete love to Rick's body in the darkness, with no cameras rolling. At these times Rick frequently heard him murmur the name "Jeff." Always when he was completely lost in passion—and often in a mournful tone.

Grimes was often away during the day, the sound of the Mercedes backing out of the garage and then returning hours later, alerting Rick to the fact. The first few times this happened, Rick tried the door and went out on the balcony unsuccessfully considering lines of escape. But he became dizzy and his heart raced each time he saw the drop off the balcony to the rocks in the ravine bed. His imprisonment seemed to be tight, and other than his host's obsessive behavior, Rick's motivation to escape was minimal. He wasn't all that outraged at what Grimes was doing with him when they were fucking, and, without clothes, he doubted he'd get very far in this desert environment even if he did manage to escape.

Only once did Rick see an opportunity to do something toward a plan to escape when he was in the mood to take any action. Once when Grimes was fucking him on the kitchen counter in the evening, Grimes turned from him and upset a bottle of red wine down his midsection and thighs. Without thinking he went off to shower it off, leaving Rick alone for a short time in the house.

Rick knew it was dangerous, but Grimes's room was the only one where he thought he could get a set of clothes to hide against the day he could escape. So, when Grimes went down the first-floor bedroom hallway, Rick followed and waited to hear the click of the bathroom door and the shower being turned on, and then he entered the bedroom and picked out the closet door and got there as fast as he could. He would have gotten there faster, but as he entered the room, his eyes were assailed by photographs set up all over the room. He thought back to the photos that had disappeared from the living room the night he'd arrived.

He looked at some in passing and they almost stopped him in his tracks. They were all of Grimes and a clothed version of the young man in the fuck photos Grimes had shown Rick that first night they'd had sex on the bear-skin rug and Rick had known they were having sex.

Time was of the essence, though, so Rick slipped into the gigantic walk-in closet and grabbed for a pullover sweater and a pair of trousers and old sneakers from near the back of the racks. They weren't his size, but he figured they'd have to do. He'd taken them to his room and hidden the clothes between the mattress and box springs and the sneakers behind a standing bureau and had gotten back into the kitchen and perched back up on the counter before Grimes returned to resume where he'd left off in the fuck.

Then one day Grimes came into the room in mid afternoon—not when it was a mealtime—and handed Rick a set of clothes. Trousers, but no briefs; a white, short-sleeved dress shirt; and a pair of socks and Rick's own loafers that Grimes had confiscated.

"My lawyer is coming for you to sign some papers," he said, not identifying further what these papers might be. "We'll have snacks and drinks in the dining room. You should be aware that I'm the only client of this lawyer, and we have a very close and full-knowledged relationship."

Rick was no dummy. He knew that meant he needn't try to enlist the lawyer to help him.

But the lawyer, Kevin Morton, ultimately did that on his own.

The three of them were sitting at the time, just starting their drinks, not much past introductions, when the telephone rang and Grimes was forced to answer it. The housekeeper was nowhere to be seen, and Rick assumed she'd been given the day off because of the change of routine. Grimes tried to end the conversation quickly, but whatever the problem was seemed to be a big one, and he got up from the table and took his cell phone into the den.

As soon as he left, the lawyer turned to Rick and said in a low voice, the concern in his tone not matching the smile he was wearing in case Grimes suddenly reappeared, "He's holding you here, isn't he? And he's molesting you."

Shocked, Rick couldn't answer. He just looked down at his hands in his lap. He even considered that this must be some sort of test.

"When I heard what Bill wanted these papers drawn up for, the first thing I thought was that he'd had a gold digger move in on him. He's been erratic for months, and I've been worried about his stability—and, frankly, his susceptibility to a young man like you. He's been through a lot in the last several months, and it's taken a toll on him—mentally and emotionally. But now that I see you, I understand. He's holding you as a sex slave, isn't he?"

"Yes," Rick finally answered in a whisper.

"Do you want to get out of here?"

Rick hesitated for a moment but then he steeled himself and murmured, "Yes, yes, of course. But I don't know—"

"I know this place can be locked down like Fort Knox, but have you tried—?"

"These are the first clothes I've had on in weeks," Rick answered in a dismal tone. "He keeps me naked and locked in a bedroom."

"Ah, I see. Yes, I see. That will be hard. I'll have to come back. Sign the papers I have today, but I'll say there are more that have to be signed. These papers will be just fine for you. The ones I bring next I'll never file. But I'll have a key for you then—and some money and a way for you to get something to wear. If you go to the back of your closet, you'll see there's a trap door with a lock."

"A trap door? You know this?"

"I supervised every step of the building of this house. Bill couldn't be bothered with the details. He'd asked for the concealed door—and others too—but I'll wager he forgot he did or could remember why he wanted them put in. I have a key that will open that door and you'll then be in the closet of another bedroom. After you've gotten the key, it will be a day or two before you can use it. When I'm able, I'll set up a meeting downtown for Bill to attend. It will be on a day that the housekeeper has off. Take what you need from his room and leave. Don't steal anything but clothes you'll need to wear and I'll see to it that you have no trouble with the law. I'll give you another key to the side door. Don't try to leave until I've come back again, though."

"How do I know you can do all of this?" Rick asked.

"I have him in the other room on the phone with someone I set up now. We couldn't be having this conversation if I hadn't thought something was going on that needed fixed. Now that I see you, it all fits."

"You've said that before," Rick said. "I don't understand."

"Have you seen the photos of Bill's son?" Morton asked.

"Yes." Rick remembered the photos he'd seen in Grimes's bedroom—the ones that probably had been moved there from the living room right after Rick arrived.

"Have you looked at yourself in the mirror?"

"You mean?"

"Yes, you are a near ringer for his son."

"What's his son's name?"

"Jeff. At least that's what his son's name was. The young man is dead."

"Jeff? Grimes was fucking his own son?"

Morton looked shocked, but his expression quickly turned to just plain weariness. "I won't ask how you supposed that. But, yes, it's true. It happens," Morton answered in a tired voice. "We did what we could in the office, but he's too powerful, too important. He was obsessed by his son. But it's why I will help you. For his sake as well as yours."

"How did his son die?"

"Suicide. Five months ago. Jumped off the balcony off his bedroom upstairs."

Rick shivered, struck by the will power—and the sense of despair—that the young man must have had to propel himself from that balcony.

"What are the papers for?"

160

"The ones I'll bring next are adoption papers. Grimes wants to adopt you. Shhh, now, here he comes back. Just sign the papers and don't ask about them. Let me get out of here as soon as possible."

True to his word, Morton came back within a week with papers for both Grimes and Rick to sign—and while the three of them were sitting in the dining room, a car smashed into the stone wall at the top of Grimes's driveway, and Grimes rushed out to see what was happening. While he was gone, making quite clear that he had set the "accident" up to occupy Grimes's attention and time, Morton went over escape directions again and gave Rick two keys, one for the trap door and one for a side door out of the house. He gave Rick something else too.

"Here's a prepaid cell phone and some money. Take them to your room right now and hide them and hurry back before Bill returns. Keep the phone with you always—my card is also taped to the back. My number is programmed in the number-one slot. Call me when you get out of here whenever you need help before you get settled again. And good luck."

The next afternoon, Grimes went into his lawyer's office at Morton's insistence to discuss the adoption procedures further, and Rick went through the trap door to the bedroom beyond, where he found his duffel bag with his own clothes, so he didn't need Grimes's clothes in larger sizes. He was dressed and out of the house and down the road and into old Santa Fe well before Bill Grimes returned home.

* * * *

For two weeks Rick laid low in a seedy gay-friendly rooming house on Galisteo Street at the fringe of the old Santa Fe plaza area. He had no idea what to do now and was considering starting to look for work in an auto repair shop. None he tried out initially needed help and at two of the them he was told, "There aren't many job openings here because there aren't nearly enough repair shops here. You should try Albuquerque. More dealers and I hear they have openings."

He waited a bit too long. He needed money to settle his account at the rooming house and also for a bus ticket to Albuquerque, which was just a couple of hours away by road but wasn't a place he'd want to try walking to. He'd already tried that once to near-disastrous results.

He needed money fast and he needed a good bit of it. He frequented a gay bar nearby, The Matador, at the corner of San Francisco and Galisteo, and every time he went in there someone tried to pick him up—and most offered him money. So, he decided this was his quickest way to a ticket out of Santa Fe.

The man was in this thirties. He was trim, darkheaded, at least partly Hispanic. He looked a little mean and dangerous, tattoos running up and down his arms and one, covering part of his well-muscled chest, was showing through the white sleeveless athletic T he was wearing over black jeans. Black boots and black-leather wrist bands with studs on them. He had a ring in an eyebrow and a big gold bead pierced in the top of his tongue near the tip.

Those were the possible downsides toward a sign of potential "bad idea" trouble. The upside was that he said, "$200, I come twice, you come as many times as you do. And I got a room." And he flashed the cash and was willing for Rick to put it in an envelope and mail it to himself before they went up to the guy's room, if that was what Rick wanted.

It sounded OK to Rick. A quick accumulation of what he needed, even if he had to take it a little rough.

The guy was all business. He had Rick on his back on the side of his bed in a room that looked far better furnished and taken care of than Rick would have expected. It was an apartment, really, with at least two bedrooms, although the door to the other bedroom off the hall was closed. The living room was more an office than a parlor. This bedroom was as good as any motel room Rick had been in before.

He told Rick he wanted Rick to come first, and he wanted to undress Rick, which he did expertly and without tearing anything, running his hands over the exposed skin as he freed it. He pushed Rick down on his back, told him to open his legs, and then stood between Rick's thighs and stripped his own clothes off, revealing the tattooing was full body and he had a ring in his navel and a super thick one in the bulb of his cock.

"You gonna give me back the $200 if you won't be bound?"

"No, I'll do that for the cash." Rick answered. He wasn't quite prepared for the two heavy frames the guy brought out, though, and put on either side of the bed, spreading Rick's arms and binding them at the wrist on one frame, and his legs by the ankles on the other one so that Rick was spread-eagled and trussed up at all four points.

Then the guy knelt between Rick's thighs and went to work on his cock. Rick quickly found out that the bead in the guy's tongue could drive his cock crazy, not only in being run up and down the length of the shaft, but because it also could be positioned at his piss slit and pushed in there in a fuck stroking motion. The guy fucked Rick's piss slit until Rick couldn't take it anymore and came in a great gush. Then the guy moved down and worked on Rick's balls and his channel opening with the bead until Rick was moaning for the cock, which, when it came, punished Rick's channel walls and prostate wonderfully with the thick ring in its bulb.

Rick came again before the guy did. After he'd finished, the guy sauntered off and came back with three chilled bottles of Corona beer. One he drank while he rolled Rick's ass up toward him so that, forcing the necks of the beer bottles up Ricks channel, he filled Rick's ass with two bottles of beer. Then he stopped up the beer from seeping out by plugging the hole with his cock again. While he fucked, he reached up and over and released Rick from his bonds, and they wound up in a close clutch, the guy's torso covering Rick's and Rick's legs hooked around his waist, as they kissed and the tattooed guy pumped, and beer seeped around his cock and down Rick's thighs.

"You're every good as in the movie," the guy muttered as he still was pumping Rick.

"What? What do you mean?"

"You're in that film, *Road to Mirage*, showing over in the gay film festival in Arizona, aren't you? You're Randy Lane."

"No, no, you have me mistaken with someone else."

"No, I wasn't sure. But I am now." He moved a hand to Rick's hip as he continued stroking, slow and deep in the soppy beer lube, driving Rick crazy with that thick ring of his. "This here birthmark gives you away. Just like in the film. It won grand prize. The film, that is. You knew that didn't you?"

"No," Rick answered, and then, on another subject. "Yes, yes, right . . . there. Oh, shit, yes. Oh fuck!"

And he came again, although the tattooed guy didn't miss a stroke in his own rhythm.

"I've been watchin' you for a week. I thought it was you. Now I know. I got you up here—$200 is a hell of a lot of money for a double fuck you know—cause I'm a filmmaker too. Different films than that one, *Journey to Mirage*. Not so artsy fartsy. Straightforward leather and such. But you're a sweet fuck on film. I wanna do a couple of forced ones. I think you'd do reluctance good. I'd like you in them."

"Sorry, not interested," Rick said, his voice still a whimper from the working over his channel was getting from the thick ring.

The guy pulled out of him and walked over and leaned against a bachelor's chest, his arm on top of the chest and his slim, well-muscled, and tattoo decorated torso tilted at a provocative angle. He looked so nasty and beautiful at the same time that Rick moaned.

"I know you'll take it and love it. You want me. You want me now."

"No, sorry. I don't want to do movies. I'm moving on."

"Sure you are. But it's OK. I'll let you think about it. I'll pay you $1,000 for the first film. More after that if the first one turns out good. We film right here. Here and in the other bedroom. Got it fixed up real nice. Some special equipment. Wanna see it?"

"No, I don't think so," Rick answered. But the truth of the matter is that maybe he did—maybe he wanted too much to see it. He forced himself to resist. He had resolved not to go down that road.

"But you'll think about it? I've got a card I'll give you and you can call me when you've decided you'll do it. I know you will. You were dynamite in the film. Sold it all by yourself. You and the other blond cutie. Wonder where he is. Ever do it together you two?"

"No."

"You bring him in and let me and the boys work you both over in a film and I'll pay you double. God, the number of dicks you took one after the other. And the vampire scene. I coulda sworn you were gonna buy the farm before that was over. You got a million-dollar ass."

"I guess I'd better go now," Rick said, "OK if I use your bathroom and take a shower before I go."

"I didn't come a second time. I paid for two."

Rick watched, wide eyed, as the guy opened a closet door and rolled out an metal apparatus looked like a saw horse with two saddles in tandem on it and leather straps on the sides front and middle. He found that the saddles were for his belly and pecs and the straps were for his arms hanging down at the sides in front and his feet and ankles bent at the sides like he was pumping a bicycle. This left his ass raised and at just the right ankle for the tattooed filmmaker to thrust inside his channel and work off his second session.

"Liked that?" he asked when he finished. "It could be in the first film if you like."

Rick indeed had liked it—he'd known for some time that he liked being bound when he did it. But the day the $200 reached him in the mail, he was out the door and on a bus for Albuquerque.

Chapter Fourteen: Albuquerque

"Ricky? Is that really you?"

"Yes, Mom, it's me. I'd doin' fine, Mom. Trying to get settled. I want you to come out when I do."

"Settled? Where are you?"

"Albuquerque. Albuquerque, New Mexico. I'd told you I wanted to settle out here and work on cars. And that I wanted you to come out too."

Silence for several seconds.

"He's gone."

"Who's gone, Mom."

No immediate response.

"Pete? Is Pete gone?"

"Yes, he left right after you did. Called me a silly old cow and cleared out."

"Mom, I tried to tell you." Rick, of course, wasn't surprised. This was the option he'd assumed Pete would take.

"Why'd you tell them all that, Ricky? The men came lookin' for Pete, but he was already gone. They said the most vile things. Why'd you tell them—?"

"Because it was true, Mom. I tried to tell you. You didn't want to see it or hear it. But Pete didn't leave because of you. He left because of me. You're better off without . . . but what did they say when they came lookin' for him? Are they lookin' for me too? Because I jumped probation?"

"No, one of the them—I think he said he was your probation officer—seemed relieved that Pete was gone. And he

167

told me that no one would pursue your case. That he was seein' to it. That as long as you kept your nose clean, it would go away. Only if you show up in the system again . . . Ricky you're not—?"

"I'm keepin' clean, Mom. And savin' money. It's nice out here. You'd like it. And there are medical jobs advertised in the papers all of the time. We could manage out here."

Silence.

"Mom?"

"We'll talk about that sometime. Thanks for callin' to tell me you ain't dead—although you took your time with it. Let me know when you've made your first million, and we'll talk about it again. Nice you got dreams still; mine ain't doin' so well. It's good to hear your voice, son. But it gets so lonely here . . . alone. I wish that Pete . . . but I gotta go now. I've got a shift to get to."

"I love you, Mom."

"That's good to hear, son."

* * * *

Albuquerque was the first place in four months that put any sort of stability into Rick's life—the first place where men weren't almost constantly putting their hands on his hips and moving in real close and telling him how nice he was, how much they wanted him—and then taking him. It wasn't all their fault, of course. Rick liked to be wanted and he liked to be taken. It had become as much an obsession with him as with them. It was only now, though, when he'd gotten to Albuquerque and found a niche where the men swirling around him weren't constantly looking at him for what he could give them, how he could scratch their sexual itch, that Rick started to see what a normal life could be and began to settle in to what every other young man enjoyed from life.

Albuquerque was the first city justifying being called that since Rick had been through Dallas, which now seemed to be a lifetime ago. Certainly then he was much less world experienced and weary than he was now. Albuquerque had an old town plaza area as most of the towns in the region did, but, as one of the first railroad hubs in the West, it also had a new city and even a few high-rise buildings. More important for Rick, it had people and automobiles and freeways. Lots of automobiles. And it had car dealerships with large service departments and auto body shops. And, as he had been told in Santa Fe, it had a shortage of auto mechanics.

Rick was able, almost immediately, to find an assistant oil monkey position at a small body shop, which led, by way of a Mexican supervisor who saw that Rick knew more about what he was doing, thanks to his auto mechanics classes in Baltimore—to Rick being recommended to the guy's cousin who worked in the service department of Miller's, a large GMC dealership on the east side of Albuquerque.

That cousin, Luis, a large-framed Mexican with a quick humor, a gift for teaching and for patience, and an encyclopedia knowledge of Chevrolets, Buicks, and Cadillacs, took Rick under his wing, and Rick began to blossom under the tutelage of the first man in his life who had no apparent sexual interests—in him or anyone else, it seemed. Luis's mistresses were all vintage automobiles, and the longer Rick worked with him, the more Rick was thusly inclined as well. The other mechanics were mostly Hispanics and mostly related to each other, but they were friendly to Rick—anyone all right with Luis being all right with them too. Although they mostly kept to themselves and rattled Spanish off to each other throughout the working day, Rick didn't feel like he was being frozen out of anything.

Rick was making good money and found a small studio apartment near the car dealership, within walking distance. Here too all he heard around him was Spanish from large Hispanic families crawling all over the neighborhood, jovially chattering to each other incessantly, hanging wash out on every available hook, and celebrating each sunset out in the courtyards with large family gatherings, guitar music, and laughter and food.

They were friendly to Rick but they more or less left him alone, and he liked it that way. He came home in the evening with service manuals under his arm and whatever else he could find on auto mechanics, and he spent his evenings poring over those. He didn't so much forget what had brought him this far from Baltimore as that he was replacing sex with the entirely different arousal of figuring out the mysteries under the hoods of automobiles.

His weekends were spent discovering Albuquerque on foot. He had been held prisoner for so long indoors, it felt good to be able to walk out into the open air, free, and able to make his own decisions and do things on whim and eat what he wanted when he wanted. He joined a gym and worked his body hard, using that to release tension. As chance would have it, the gym was on the fringes of the Central Avenue gay district, which he had also found early in his strolls and had had a little trouble resisting exploring further. At the gym he saw hookups that invariably gave him pause and twitched his butt in memory, but he was determined to take on a new life, revolving around cars that needed help, and he resisted. He was frequently hit on when he first started at the gym, but soon the regulars got the message and left him to himself.

The dealership—in addition to two others—was owned by three brothers. Rick almost never saw the oldest brother, Ted, who was running the Ford dealership. Roy, who managed this one, was the epitome of a used car salesman—at the door with a hand out and a big smile on his face whenever a potential customer was walking along the street. Behind the scenes he was a demanding boss who Luis and the other older guys in the service department continually warned would be a good one to stay the hell away from. That didn't pose a problem. Roy never came into the service department, and, the men joked, probably didn't know where the hood latch was on any of the cars he sold.

The younger brother, Jess, seemed to just float around from dealership to dealership, although Luis had told Rick that he managed the car empire's smaller, exclusively foreign sports car resales dealership on the better side of the town.

Jess was the "golden touch" brother from, Luis told Rick, a younger wife than the other two brothers. He was a lot better looking and much trimmer and significantly younger than the other two. He wore cowboy shirts and a ten-gallon hat much more convincingly than either of his two brothers did, and his smile was more convincing too. When he shook your hand he was looking into your eyes with pale blue ones of his own that made you happy and tingly all at once. He irritated Roy noticeably when he came around the GMC dealership in his vintage baby-blue Cadillac convertible, because he could glide through the showroom in those tooled cowboy boots of his and sell five cars effortlessly.

Everyone wanted to be his friend. He was a poster child for success, and he was always being asked when he was going to run for city council. He often brought his model-perfect blonde wife in with him, his three perfect tow-headed children following along like ducks in a row, and everyone in the dealership—except Roy—snapped to and brightened up in his wake. Every family visit was like a video commercial for him running for office.

And, unlike Roy, Jess didn't stint on the service department. Whenever he showed up, he'd end up in the service department, he and Luis peering under the hood of Jess's beloved Cadillac convertible and worshiping this and that in the engine compartment. He had time to talk to each of the guys in the service area, to ask about their families and to shake their hands. He was especially attentive to Rick and was happy discussing auto parts with him, careful not to rub it in that he knew more than Rick did, and each time leaving Rick knowing more about the automotive industry than he had before Jess had walked through. Once even, Luis had come into work early, as he always did, to find both Rick and Jess already there. Luis spied four legs under the chassis of a car, and both young men came out from underneath it with grease on their hands and their faces and flush from the celebration of, together, having located the source of an oil leak and stopping it up.

Everything was going just fine until Rick saw the quarter-page ad in the Sunday paper. It was for a film series showing at a local club. Sponsored by the local gay community, through an organization called Closet Cinema, the top-rated films of the year's Mirage gay film festival were going to be shown, with short film runs of each, over a two-week period. Without thinking, Rick looked at the list of films being shown. *Journey to Mirage* wasn't hard to find. As the festival grand winner, it was at the top of the list. There were more than a dozen showings he could catch at a local club called the Albuquerque Mining Company. Rick knew where it was—in the middle of the Central Avenue gay district. He hadn't gone inside ever, but he'd been tempted to.

He told himself he wasn't tempted to go see the film that had taken so much out of him and yet fulfilled so many fantasies of his. But even then he knew he would.

He picked a Thursday afternoon, taking off from work—the first day he'd ever asked for, so Luis saw no reason not to give it to him. Rick reasoned that there would be fewer patrons at the club then. He could slip in, see the film, and slip out again.

The film was mesmerizing. He relived every moment, every fantasy, every fuck. He was both exhausted and drained and, at the same time, keyed up and his balls aching from buildup, the need for release, as he came out of the movie and into the blinding light. His eyes were having trouble adjusting to the glare and he almost stumbled into someone standing firmly in his line of exit.

"Um, sorry," he muttered as he moved to the left to get around the figure. But the figure moved with him, and Rick looked down and saw cowboy boots he recognized and his new world collapsed around his now-leaden feet.

"It was you. That really was you. You're Randy Lane."

Rick looked up into those pale-blue eyes of Jess Miller, and he felt like dissolving into the baking sidewalk.

172

"Uh. No, not me . . . not—"

"Come with me, please." Jess had him firmly in a hold on his arm and was marching him toward a nearby parking garage. Rick followed along in shock, imaging all sorts of bad outcomes from this. Exposure. Worse, being hauled back to stand before Luis and Roy for the accusation and the very public dress down and firing.

Rick saw the bull horn ornament grinning at him from the front of the Cadillac convertible as he was hustled up the ramp. Jess opened the passenger side of the door and pushed Rick in and went around to the other side and drove at high speed down to the ticket booth and then at higher speed through the city.

It didn't take Rick long, though, to see that they weren't driving toward the GMC dealership. Maybe the auto group had some sort of corporate offices? Or was the police department in this direction? But Rick couldn't figure out what the police would have to do with anything. He hadn't broken any laws or anything. And he hadn't misrepresented himself to get the job. He hadn't even applied for a job at the GMC dealership; he'd been recommended and taken on faith. Taken on faith, Rick thought, and then he gave a nervous little laugh. Would Luis have taken him on if he had known about Rick's past? And there was probably an outstanding warrant on him back in Maryland. But he hadn't misrepresented himself. His name wasn't Randy Lane; it was Rick Hernandez. And he was a damn good auto mechanic now. He was doing the job he was being paid for.

"Mr. Miller," he said in a low voice, trying to break the frosty silence that had hung over them from the beginning. Maybe trying to come up with an explanation that would make it all go away.

"Shut up and be quiet, Rick—or Randy, or whoever you are. Just shut up. I had no idea. I . . ." But then he shut up himself.

They were out of the city now, driving out onto the ranges, where the ranches were starting to get spaced farther apart. He turned onto a dirt road and they were riding between two spreads with cattle on either side and back into the scrub a couple of miles farther. The road ended at a small compound with an adobe house and a few outbuildings. The house didn't look derelict, but it didn't exactly look like anyone lived there now, either. The outbuildings were in a bit worse shape, except for a garage that looked fairly new.

Jess drove around to the back of the house, to where the Cadillac couldn't be seen from the front, and he turned off the motor and sat there for a moment, trembling—Rick assumed from rage—for a moment and looking down at the hands in his lap, which were also trembling slightly.

"Mr. Miller. That isn't me now. I'm a good mechanic."

"I . . . asked . . . you not to speak," Jess hissed through almost closed lips. And then he turned and looked into Rick's eyes. And Rick saw the wildness in the eyes and he saw something else, something all too familiar.

Like a cat leaping following an eternity of watching and twitching its tail, Jess had leaned into Rick and grabbed the hair at the back of Rick's head and snapped his head back and was at Rick's mouth with his own, greedily possessing it, while his other hand was fumbling with Rick's belt buckle and zipper and was digging for Rick's cock.

Mere seconds later, Jess's face was in Rick's lap and Jess was slurping on Rick's cock. He was pushing Rick's briefs and jeans off his legs with a hand that then dug under his balls, searching for Rick's channel. Rick moaned and rolled his hips up to give Jess's long, strong fingers access. Rick's hands were on the back of Jess's head, holding him and guiding him in the suck.

It had been so long, and the movie had keyed him up so high. Rick had told himself he didn't need this anymore. But it had been a lie. He'd lied to himself.

"Mr. Miller," he murmured. "Oh, god. Oh, shit. Yesss. Ohhh FUCK!"

It had been so obvious. Why hadn't he known? He was there. Jess Miller was there. How would he have recognized

Rick in the movie, if he hadn't been there himself, watching the movie?

"In the back. Now." Jess said, his voice thick with want.

"We shouldn't," Rick objected to weakly. "You don't want to . . . your family." But he went no further. He wanted it. And Jess was a wild man. Rick knew Jess had to have it. And here, now, so did Rick.

Jess was fumbling with the buttons on Rick's cowboy shirt, nearly ripping it off his back. Jess's teeth went to an exposed nipple and Rick yelped at the bite. "Now!" Jess demanded. He was out of the car, dragging Rick with him with one hand and tearing at his own clothes with the other then shoving him into the backseat.

Miller sat on the trunk of the car, legs spread and descending into the backseat compartment, the soles of his feet, still clad in the cowboy boots, leveraging off the cushy seat cushion, while he slow pumped his cock up into Rick's enveloping mouth cavity. When he couldn't take any more, he pulled Rick up from between his legs, reversed their position, with Rick belly down on the lid of the trunk, head pointed at the tailpipes. Jess stood, reversed on the backseat, crouched over Rick's hips and pumped and pumped and pumped until, giving a little cry of release, he collapsed onto Rick's back, where they both lay, panting and murmuring wonders of the fuck to each other.

"Come into the house. Let me put the Caddie in the garage and then come into the house with me."

"I don't know . . . we shouldn't have—"

"I'll put the Caddie away and then we'll go into the house."

Both still naked except for their boots, Jess led Rick in through the back door. They entered a well-appointed kitchen that belied the aged look of the outside of the house. Beyond that was a living and dining room combined that was furnished well and was clean and uncluttered. A small hall to the right gave access to two bedrooms, one on the front of the house and one on the back, with a bathroom between them.

"It's nice, Mr. Miller. But I don't understand—"

"Come into the back bedroom. I want to show you your bed."

My bed. The phrase shot through Rick's brain, and he was suddenly thinking of Bill Grimes. And his blood ran cold.

But Jess's blood wasn't cold. He was still very much in heat and, Rick could clearly see, very much in erection again.

The bed was a brass headboarded one, just like so many others Rick had known. It creaked and groaned just as badly as the one at the Big C ranch had while Jess missionary fucked Rick with animalistic fury and intensity—and with great stamina—while Rick reached for the brass pillars in the headboard and hung on for dear life, enough into the fuck, though, to meet every upward thrust of Jess's cock with a downward thrust of his own hips.

An eternity later, when they were laying in each other's arms, the sweat still pouring off both, Jess spoke through heaving breaths.

"The place is mine. I keep it for my . . . for my men. But it will be just for you now. You won't have to work anymore. You can stay out here and I'll bring everything to you. It'll be good. There's a TV and the radio. And I'll bring you any books you need and anything else. We'll have a ball."

"Sounds like . . . like paradise," Rick answered back, thinking that it sounded more like yet another mirage, yet another prison. "I'll have to go back to town, though, to get my things and to let Luis know—"

"I'll take care of Luis. He'll understand. He told me all along you'd probably be a great lay. Said he'd make it happen for me. Imagine my surprise when I saw you in that movie. Went back three times, not believing my eyes. And then, today, there you were."

"Luis? He procures . . . for you?"

"Shush. I don't think I'll need anyone else for some time now. God, you've got a sweet ass. And that movie. We'll have to buy a copy. I want to do so much of that with you."

"Uh, I'll want to go back to my apartment for my things, and in a few days. . . . but now maybe we should get dressed and . . ."

"Now? Not yet. I want you again."

Rick groaned, but when Jess nudged him, he rolled onto his stomach himself. And he himself reached for his butt cheeks and spread them for Jess. He too wanted it again now. He had only been fooling himself about being able to go without it. Jess's cock was only average. But it was there. Fully erect once more for him. And Jess's body was so beautiful.

* * * *

Rick stood at the third-floor window of his studio apartment and watched Jess drive off in his Cadillac convertible. He exhaled a long breath, not realizing that he had been holding his breath tightly in his chest for the entire ride back into town. He had been agreeing to everything Jess was saying about where they went from here, using one- or two-word phrases and a quiet voice—while inside he was screaming and wildly revolving in his mind what he had to do—what he wanted, who he wanted it from, assessing every thought for honesty and feasibility.

He was standing at the window to make sure Jess was gone.

He then searched around for the calling card he'd kept, took out his prepaid cell phone—the one that Bill Grimes's lawyer had given him, and dialed a number in Santa Fe.

"Yes?" the sleepy voice answered on the other end. Rick heard what he thought were groans and laughter in the background.

"Hello. It's me, Ricky—the guy you know as Randy Lane. You said I could call."

"Ah, yes, the sweet-assed movie star," the tattooed filmmaker said on the other end. It wasn't a putdown. He said it was a great deal of feeling and respect. "You ready to come do a film? I can send someone for you if you'll tell me where—"

"I'm still thinking about it. But maybe you can help me out with something and then maybe I can help you out with something."

"Shoot. What do you want?"

"You're in films. I thought maybe you can find out for me where Doug Groton, the producer of the *Journey* film, is and how to contact him."

"Sure, kid, all of the gay filmmakers know where Groton is now. You put him on the map. He's still in Arizona. They liked his film so much that they've kept him there at the festival office and he's putting together some more films for their festival next year. Got a number for him right here if you want to hold."

The filmmaker was off and the background noise was clearer now. The unmistakably sound of rough sex, and of someone maybe being taken without full willingness. Rick shuddered, but he held on to the cell phone.

The tattooed filmmaker returned and gave Rick Groton's number in Arizona. "So, how's about it? A little tied up here for a couple of more hours"—this was met in the background noise by a hearty laugh—"but we can set something back up by tonight, say about ten, if you're interested in getting started. I can send someone for you."

"I'm still thinking about it, thanks. I'll call you back in a day or two." He didn't bother to tell the guy he wasn't in Santa Fe anymore.

The next call was to Arizona, and Douglas Groton answered on the third ring.

"Great to hear from you, Rick," he said in response to Rick's voice. "Glad you called. We're a hit. They love you on movie screens coast to coast."

"That's why I called, Mr. Groton. Would you . . . do you have any interest on me coming back to you and doing some more films?"

"That would be great, Rick." And Rick could tell by the inflection in Groton's voice that it *would* be great indeed. "Dumbest thing I did letting you go. They love you out here. Everyone's clambering to have you in their films. So, a change in mind?"

"No, more just not fighting it anymore. If, of course, the money's good."

"For you, Rick, the money'll be very good, very good indeed. I can send you some to travel on, if you need it."

"Uh, thanks, some up front would be good, but I have enough to travel on." Rick didn't want Groton to have an address to send money to. "Can you give me an address to show up to?"

Groton did. And then, before they signed off, Rick asked him another question.

"Uh, is Billy Dan there with you still?"

Groton laughed down the line. "Nope. He and Howard ran off on me two days after you did. Threw me for a loop, it did. Not because I needed Billy much anymore; the filming was complete and I was in the editing phase. It was rough doing without Howard. And I certainly had guessed on Howard wrong. I wouldn't have bet he even had a dick. Good film editor, though. Him, I missed at that point. Lefty was bad-ass angry and pulling his pube hairs out over the loss of Billy, but I figure Howard will dump him for a new computer and Billy will be crawling back to Lefty one of these days."

Rick hoped not, but he decided not to get into that with Groton.

Groton continued. "Oh, but Spike's back out here. I know he'll be glad to see you too. And I got some more guys like Spike. The film I'm gonna do next is a little, I guess you'd say aggressive. But you'll be perfect in that. You always showed best when it was a little rough and the guy was a bruiser.

Viewers eat this vulnerable tail business up. Made you look so much more into it—and you really enjoyed that, I could tell."

Had he really enjoyed that the best, Rick wondered, as he put the cell phone back in the duffel. Maybe he had, if he was honest with himself. But he'd rarely had an alternative. On that there was mostly Phil that he remembered. So, he wasn't at all sure what he liked best.

He didn't dwell on that, though. Packed and having informed his landlord he was leaving immediately and having called the furniture store and told them to come back and pick up the few things he still had on approval, Rick left the apartment and walked into town, to the bus station, and waited for the next bus to Phoenix. He made sure he didn't pass the GMC dealership on his way.

Chapter Fifteen: Phoenix

The bus trip was a good nine hours, with all the stops in small towns, between Albuquerque and Phoenix, and it had been a couple of hours after dark before Rick had gotten to the bus station and boarded one headed for Phoenix. The quiet hours of blackness, punctuated by the lights of cars and towns passed bouncing off the ceiling and seat tops of the nearly empty vehicle gave him much time, between fitful snoozes, to contemplate where he was going.

He was going to Mirage, it would seem, on a much-interrupted trip there. And he was almost there. But what would be there when he reached it? Was it what he had seen off in the distance there when he'd started out from Baltimore? Was it the ultimate release and escape for him that he had thought then? No, certainly not. He was as much a prisoner now to other men as he had been to Tony and Pete—and then Douglas Groton—back in Baltimore.

The oasis out there in the desert, his destination, had changed in character and magnitude as he had approached it. If anything, it had become more hopeless and sinister the closer he got. And it had become smaller, less glorified and inviting.

And was it really there at all?

So, why was he on a bus headed for Phoenix and, ultimately, Mirage? So near, and yet it seemed as far away now as it had ever been.

There were only two things he knew how to do: fix cars and entertain men with sex. He wanted to do the first, but

181

it would be hard to get a job at that in Phoenix. Worse than not having any references, it wouldn't take much effort to find that he'd worked at Miller's as close as Albuquerque. What would they say about him there when asked? That this Rick guy just didn't show up for work one day? Would Luis have something more damning to say to punish him? Or would Jess take the information and come for him—folding Rick right back into a prison, no matter how pleasant Jess's cocking was?

No, even to be able to be fixing cars now, Rick needed a new life—and time. Only money brought that. And the only way Rick could think of to get the money he'd need—to live, let alone follow any dream—was to use his other skills for a while.

Rick would see how much money Groton would actually give him and how soon he could get out of the business altogether.

Beyond that, though, just as the mirage out there had reformed and not come significantly closer, Rick had grown and changed too. He would take more control. He wouldn't be a prisoner to anyone again like he had been before. And he had never been completely passive to begin with. He had escaped what was both the physical and mental pull of a series of dominant men: Tony, Pete, Groton, Bill Grimes, and Jess Miller. Rick would go back with Groton—and truth be known, that long, long cock of his was something that Rick looked forward to—but now the footing would be more equal.

Rick would make films with him, but if Groton thought it would be rough, leather films, he was sadly mistaken. Rick had already had that offer in Santa Fe, and had walked away from it.

It was nearly dawn when Rick's bus pulled into Phoenix. He found the nearest hotel that looked like he could afford it and wasn't a flop house—he was not in the mood for drama or being hit on—and slept into the afternoon. Then he found out which city bus would take him to Sky Harbor airport.

His trip to the airport was about as frustrating to him as anything he had experienced on the long road from Baltimore. He was trying to rent a car—a cheap one, if he could. He had no idea where Mirage was in relation to Phoenix. Just in the same state. But he figured he'd need a car to get there. There had been no destination under "M" on the board in the bus station other than Mesa.

He probably should have called instead of showing up in person, although, ultimately that was unlikely to work either. The attendants at the car rental kiosks were all smiles until they saw how young he looked—and that he had a Maryland driver's license that looked fake to them, even though it wasn't. The clincher, though, was that he didn't have a credit card. He wanted to pay in cash. Suddenly there were no rental cars available at Sky Harbor.

He could have slit his wrists right there until one hopeful rental associate said, "Hey, I heard you say you wanted to drop the car off in Mirage. It's really El Mirage, you know, and it's just twenty miles up highway 60 from here. Why don't you just go to the bus station and get a bus headed for Las Vegas? You can get a ticket for only as far as El Mirage."

Rick was grateful for the information and felt stupid that he already was almost standing on top of what Groton and everyone else had said was Mirage, but he didn't have the energy this afternoon to do more than get back to his hotel on the city bus. He had half a notion to call Groton and tell him to come pick him up—it could be the first test of the balance of control. But he was too tired and keyed up now to do that today.

He heard the buzzing from the hotel corridor. The walls were the thickness of tissue paper in this hotel. The buzzing continued as he unlocked and entered his room. The sound was coming from his duffel bag.

Rick fished through the duffel to the bottom and came up with the ringing cell phone—the one that Bill Grime's lawyer had given him.

"Who the hell would call me on this," he muttered as he looked for button that would put it on speaker. "I've never used this."

"Rick? Rick Hernandez? I've been trying to reach you for hours. Almost decided you'd ditched the phone."

Rick muttered something—enough for Kevin Morton, Grime's lawyer, to know someone had picked up.

"It's Kevin Morton, Bill Grimes's lawyer."

"How'd you know where I was?" Rick answered in confusion.

"It's my cell phone, remember? I gave it to you. I have the number. You haven't called."

"Uh, no, I'm doin' OK, thanks."

"I didn't call to find out how you were doing. I called to inform you that Bill Grimes is dead."

"Dead? I don't under . . . hey, wait. I had nothin' to do with anything like that. I left right away for Albuquerque. I've got people there who can say where I've—"

Rick went silent and was beginning to shake and sweat. Did he really have anyone in Albuquerque who could or would alibi him for anything? He couldn't go back to the Miller's auto dealers and the Hispanic families in his neighborhood probably never really saw him in the first place. But there was his landlord. Yes, there at least—

"No, no, you don't understand. Grimes committed suicide. Lots of us saw it coming and it was clear he did it himself. I'm calling because you are his heir. And there aren't any contenders."

"His heir? I don't understand. You said . . . the adoption papers."

"No, no. The first set of papers you signed made you his heir—everything he owned. And Bill Grimes was a very wealthy man. I saw his end coming—and, under the circumstances, although I couldn't do much about it while he was alive, I don't regret not trying to prevent him from crashing and burning nor do I regret helping him set up the paperwork to assign an heir before he did so. It was what he wanted anyway. He had the will drawn up before and separately from the adoption procedures. And if there are questions, I'll vouch that he wanted to adopt you. And I've kept his memos of intent. Anyone who sees you and knew his son can see how he would attach to you. And frankly, as long as he's gone, not many in his world will look too far into anything. We all saw it coming and saw the change in him. This is clearly what he wanted."

"Uh, I'm not sure what to say. Could I call you back tomorrow or something. This needs to sink in."

"Yes, yes, of course. I understand it's a shock. But there will be no irregularities. I was his lawyer and the paperwork is air tight and there are no contenders. I can handle this for you, if you like, or find a very good lawyer for you for your own, if you wish. You'll have to come to Santa Fe, of course—sometime soon. You can come anytime you want. There will be a house for you to stay in and a couple of cars to use—they are yours anyway."

"OK, thanks. Let me sleep on this. I'll call you tomorrow. Do I have your—?"

Morton laughed. "You really have been thrown off the beam, haven't you? When I gave you the cell phone, I told you my number was programmed in. Just hit the number one button in the address file."

Rick was shaking when he rang off. He needed to lay down. No, scratch that, he thought. He needed a stiff drink.

He left the hotel room and, impatient with the slowness of the elevator to respond, bounded down the four flights to the ground level. He stood out in front of the hotel momentarily, indecisive on which way to turn, and eventually, because he needed that drink now more than ever, just turned right and started walking down the store fronts of a strip mall. He was looking in the windows, at the displays, but not really seeing anything—just glancing long enough to think, "Nope, not a bar."

He stopped at the window of a photography shop. Phil looked up and stared back at him through the window, incredulous.

It was Phil, not knowing why Rick was a zombie, who managed to guide Rick to a nearby bar and not press him with any questions until Rick had downed his first shot of Bourbon.

"I told you I was thinking of opening a photography shop in the Southwest somewhere," Phil said in answer to Rick's question. "This seemed as good a place as any. So, what are you doing here? Still with Groton? I saw that the movie was finished and won the grand prize at the festival. So, are you out here with Groton and working on another?"

"I left Groton in Amarillo, Texas, Phil. Billy Dan left him soon after that too. We weren't needed anymore. He had our part in the can."

"And he hasn't paid you?"

"Not much yet."

"Not yet? You are in contact with him then?"

"Yes."

"And he's here in Phoenix?"

"In El Mirage."

"Ah." Phil knew how close El Mirage was to Phoenix. "You on your way there now? You going to hook up with him again?"

"Yes. Uh, no, maybe not. Oh, I don't know." Not until now had it dawned on Rick that this inheritance changed everything. Suddenly the playing field was opened to him. His options had expanded. But that meant once more that he had to choose between goals.

"So, have you reached your goals, Phil?" he said, turning on Phil to make up for his confused thoughts. "You own that camera shop, do you?" Phil had drawn blood, and Rick's defensive response was unmistakable.

"No, I just work in the camera shop," Phil answered. "But good goals don't usually come without pain and effort. And the one goal that became more important to me than my

186

dream of my own shop turned out to be a mirage in itself. So, I guess you could say that so far I'm a loser."

Rick didn't respond to that. He was silent, the color rising in his face. Stung by the knowledge that Phil was talking about him as a goal that had vanished in the sands.

"It's your life, of course," Phil said, continuing when Rick had gone silent. "My view hasn't changed. I still think that Groton and those movies and where you think you are headed beyond Phoenix are all mirages. That they are empty goals that will vanish whenever you think you are achieving them. But I'll let you see the truth of that by yourself. The most I can say is that I think you are better than all of that." He laughed then and downed his own glass of bourbon and stood up from the stool. "One thing that wasn't a mirage, though. You were worth my tossing away that job for, even for the short time we had. You are undoubtedly the best lover I ever had. I haven't found anything to satisfy me in that way since."

Phil was on his feet and preparing to turn to the door. He had already thrown down the price of the drinks, assuming that Rick couldn't pay. But then Rick put out a hand and grabbed his arm.

"I have a hotel room just down the block," he said. That was all he had to say.

After they had spent themselves fucking, Rick on his back, legs wrapped around Phil's thighs, and Phil full length on top of him, trapping Rick's hands in his and his forehead plastered to Rick's and holding Rick's eyes captive of his to grasp and appreciate every nuance of Rick's expression during the taking, Phil rolled off to the side. They maintained their embrace though, and laid in each other's arms, panting as their breath came back under control and luxuriating in a fully satisfying experience for both of them—something wondrous they whispered to each other before Rick spoke more seriously.

"Is Phoenix where you really want to be? Sort of flat and too big, if you ask me. If you owned a shop, do you think you'd like to have it in Santa Fe?"

"Don't know. Santa Fe is a bit rich for my blood."

"So, you could charge more for your cameras and film and get away with it."

"I suppose. But it's not something I have to think about for the next twenty years or so."

"Maybe, maybe not. Did I tell you that I'm rich. Maybe even a millionaire?"

"Rich, but you don't know how rich?" Phil laughed.

"Well, I haven't counted it yet."

"I'll bite. What will you be doing in Santa Fe?"

"I'll own a service garage—maybe even a dealership. I'm sort of partial to Toyotas."

"And where would we live?"

"Oh, I have a very nice house in Santa Fe—in the hills overlooking the old town. And a Mercedes and an SUV. A BMW, I think."

"You think? You've never seen it?"

"Just snatches as it was driving away. But it's just waiting for me there."

"Nice dream. But you're only twenty miles from your goal—from El Mirage. What about that dream?"

"Not so interesting now," Rick answered. "Someone I really love told me once that it is only a mirage. There's no there there."

"I love the way you dream," Phil murmured. He was heated up again and was working Rick's cock with a hand.

"And I love the way you fuck. Dreams can wait. I can't wait much longer for more of you, please."

About the Author

Habu is one of the pen names of a former supersonic spy jet pilot, intelligence agent, male model, movie actor, and diplomat. An American, he is a published mainstream novelist and short story writer under another name and in another dimension of his life, but he has written or cowritten (with Sabb) over 400 published short stories and numerous published erotica e-books, primarily of gay fiction but also memoir, straight fiction and ménage fiction. His hand and creative writing can be seen in stories and books by habu, sr71plt, shabbu, and Stephen Kessel—among unrevealed others that might surprise readers. The fictionalized GM memoir "Flying High" is loosely based on his life experiences.

BOOKS BY HABU
Sailorboy
Cairo Surrender
Fetish Galore!
Homeward Bound
Journey to Mirage
Choke Hold
The Sporting Life
Platres Conclave
Grab Bag

www.BarbarianSpy.com